Please return on or before the latest date above.
You can renew online at *www.kent.gov.uk/libs*
or by telephone 08458 247 200

CUSTOMER SERVICE EXCELLENCE

Libraries & Archives

00884\DTP\RN\07.07   LIB 7

First Published in Great Britain 2003
Large Print Edition 2008
Harlequin Mills & Boon Limited,
Eton House, 18-24 Paradise Road,
Richmond, Surrey TW9 1SR

© Jessica Steele 2003

ISBN: 978 0 263 20687 6

Set in Times Roman 15½ on 17 pt.
82-0908-62093

Printed and bound in Great Britain
by Antony Rowe Ltd, Chippenham, Wiltshire

Queens of Romance

*A collection of bestselling novels
by the world's leading romance writers*

Dear Reader

I have had a long and happy association with Mills and Boon. It began with that first lunch with Frances and Pat, then the chief editor and chief copy editor of the company. There were many trips to London for lunch after that; all splendid and most joyful affairs.

Apart from leaving home to journey to London, I have made many other trips in relation to my writing. I have just returned from Switzerland where I have been doing a little research for my next book—my eighty-seventh for Mills and Boon. It was an especially enjoyable trip, and such a pleasure—as is being an author for such a wonderful company.

Jessica Steele

A
PAPER MAR

BY

JESSICA STEELE

MILLS & BOON®
Pure reading pleasure™

CHAPTER ONE

LYDIE was in worried mood as she drove her car in the direction of Buckinghamshire to her family home. Something was wrong, very wrong. She had known it the moment she had heard her mother's voice over the telephone.

Her mother never rang her. It was always she who rang her mother. Lydie had held back from asking what was wrong—her mother would tell her soon enough. 'I want you to come home straight away,' Hilary Pearson had said almost before their greeting was over.

'I'm coming next Tuesday for Oliver's wedding on Saturday,' Lydie reminded her.

'I want you here before then,' her mother stated sharply.

'You need my help in some way?'

'Yes, I do!'

'Oliver...' Lydie began.

'It has nothing to do with your brother or his wedding!' her mother snapped sharply. 'The Ward-Watsons are more than capable of seeing to it that their only daughter gets married in style.'

'Dad!' Lydie cried in alarm. 'He's not ill?' She thought the world of her father. She occasionally felt that fate had dealt him a raw deal when it had selected her sometimes acid-tongued mother for the mild-mannered man.

'Physically he's as fit as he always has been.'

'You're saying he has a mental health problem?' Lydie asked in alarm.

'Good heavens, no! He's just worried, not sleeping well, he's…'

'What's he worried about?'

There was a moment or two of silence. 'I'll tell you that when you get here,' her mother eventually replied.

'Why can't you tell me now?' Lydie pressed.

'When you get here.'

'You can't leave it there!' Lydie protested.

'I'm certainly not going to discuss it over the phone.'

Oh, for heaven's sake! Who did her mother think was listening in? 'I'll ring Dad at his office,' Lydie decided.

'Don't you dare! He's not to know I've been in touch with you.'

'But…'

'And anyway, your father no longer has an office.'

'He…' What the Dickens was going on?

'Come home,' her mother demanded crisply—and put down the phone.

Lydie's initial reaction was to dial her mother straight back. A second later, though, and she accepted that to ring her would be a waste of time. If her mother had made up her mind to tell her nothing, Lydie knew from experience that she would get nothing more from her until her mother was ready.

Despite her mother's 'Don't you dare' Lydie dialled her father's business number. She need not tell him anything of her mother's call, just say she'd called to say hello prior to seeing him again when she arrived at her lovely old home next week.

A few minutes later and Lydie began to feel seriously worried herself. There was no ringing out tone from her father's firm; his number was a ceased number. '…your father no longer has an office' her mother had said.

At that point Lydie put down the phone and went in search of the woman whose employ she was due to leave next week. Though Donna was more like the sister she had never had than an employer. She found her in the sitting room with one-year-old Sofia and three-year-old Thomas. They looked such a contented family and Lydie knew she was going to feel quite a pang when she left the family she had been nanny to for the past three years.

Donna looked up. 'Did I hear the phone?' she asked with a smile.

'My mother rang.'

'Everything all right at home?'

'How would you feel if I left a week earlier than we said?'

'Today?' Donna queried, her smile disappearing. 'I'd hate it.'

'You'll be fine on your own; I know you will,' Lydie assured her bracingly.

That had been some hours ago. Lydie drove into her home village and realised she had been an infrequent visitor just lately to the home she so loved. Beamhurst Court was in her blood, and it had been a dreadful wrench to leave Beamhurst five years ago when at the age of eighteen she had gone to begin her career as a nanny.

Her first job had not worked out when the husband had started to get ideas about his children's nanny that had not been in her terms of employment. She had left to go and look after Thomas, Donna and Nick Cooper's first child, while they followed their careers.

Donna had suffered a quite terrible bout of the baby-blues following the birth of her second child, Sofia. While she was surfacing from that she had started to get very depressed at the thought of returning to work. It had been her husband Nick who had suggested that unless she desperately wanted to keep on with her career, given that they would not be able to afford a nanny and would have to let Lydie go, they could otherwise manage quite adequately without her income.

'What do you think?' Donna had asked Lydie. 'Which would make you happier?'

Donna thought, but not for very long. 'I've always felt a bit of a pang at missing out on Thomas's first couple of years,' she answered. That, simply, decided the matter.

Lydie had been due to leave next Tuesday, when she went home for her brother's wedding the following Saturday. She knew it would not be long before she found another job but, having been so happy with the Coopers, and on edge most of the time with her previous employers, she was in no rush to accept the first job offered.

She turned her car in through the gates of Beamhurst Court and love for the place welled up in her. She stopped for a brief while just to sit and look her fill. Beamhurst would one day be handed down to her brother, she had always known that, but that did not stop the feeling of joy she felt each time she came back.

But her mother was waiting for her, and Lydie started up her car again and proceeded slowly up the drive, starting to get anxious again about what it was that worried her father so, and what it was that caused his business telephone line to be unobtainable.

She left her car on the drive, knowing that her father was her first priority. She would not be looking for a new job until she knew what was happening here. Using her house key, she let herself in and went in search of her parents.

She did not have to look far; her mother was in the hall talking to Mrs Ross, their housekeeper. Lydie kissed her mother and passed a few pleasantries with Mrs Ross, whereupon her mother said they would have afternoon tea in the drawing room.

While Mrs Ross went kitchenwards Lydie followed her slim stiff-backed mother into the drawing room. 'You took your time getting here!' her mother complained tartly, turning to close the door behind them.

'I had to pack. Since I was leaving anyway there didn't seem much point in going back next week to collect my belongings,' Lydie answered, but had more important matters on her mind. 'What's going on? I rang Dad's office and—'

'I specifically told you not to!' her mother interrupted her waspishly.

'I wouldn't have mentioned you'd phoned me! If I'd had the chance! His number's unobtainable. Where's Dad now? You said he no longer has an office. But that's impossible. For years—'

'Your father no longer has an office because he no longer has a business!' Hilary Pearson cut her off.

Lydie's lovely green eyes widened in amazement. 'He no longer...!' she gasped, and wanted to protest, to believe that her mother was joking, but the tight-lipped look on her parent's face showed that her mother saw no humour in the situation. 'He's *sold* the business?' Lydie questioned.

'Sold it! It was taken away from him!'

'Taken! You mean—stolen?' Lydie asked, reeling.

'As good as. The bank wanted their pound of flesh—they took everything. They're after this house too!'

'After Beamhurst!' Lydie whispered, horrified.

'Oh, we all know you're besotted with the place; you always have been. But unless *you* can do something about it, they'll force us to sell it to pay them their dues!'

'Unless I...' Already Lydie's head was starting to spin.

'Your father paid out enough for your expensive education—totally wasted! It's time for you to pay him something back.'

Lydie was well aware that she was a big disappointment to her mother. Without bothering to take into account her daughter's extremely shy disposition, Hilary Pearson had been exceedingly exasperated that, when Lydie's exam results were little short of excellent, she should take on what her mother considered the menial work of a nanny. Lydie still had moments of shyness, and was still a little reserved, but she had overcome that awful shyness to a very large extent.

She stared at her mother incredulously. Pay back! She hadn't asked to be sent to an expensive boarding school. That had been her mother's idea. 'There's that few thousand pounds that Grandmother left me. Dad can have that, of course, but...'

'You can't touch that until you're twenty-five. And in any case we need far more than that if we're not to be thrown out like paupers.' Thrown out! Of Beamhurst! No! Lydie could not believe that. Could not believe that things were as bad as that. Beamhurst Court had been in the Pearson family for generations. It was unthinkable that they should let it go out of the family. But her mother was going angrily on, 'I've told your father that if the house has to go, then so shall I!'

'*Mother!*' Lydie exclaimed, on the instant angry too that when, by the look of it, her father should need his wife's support most, she should threaten to walk out on him. Anything else Lydie might have added, however, remained unsaid when Mrs Ross brought in a tray of tea and set it down.

While Hilary Pearson presided over the delicate tea cups, Lydie made herself calm down. Her last visit home had been four months ago now, she realised with surprise. Though with Donna only then starting to get better, but still feeling down and unable to cope a lot of the time, she had wanted her near at hand should everything became too much for her.

Taking the cup and saucer her mother handed to her, Lydie sat down opposite her, and then quietly asked, 'What has been happening? Everything was fine the last time I was home.'

'Six months ago,' her mother could not resist, seemingly oblivious that she was out by a couple of months. 'And everything was far from fine, as you call it.'

'I didn't see any sign...'

'Because your father didn't want you to. He said there was no need for you to know. That it would only worry you unnecessarily, and that he'd think of something.'

It had been going on all this while? And she had known nothing about it! She tried to concentrate on the matter in hand. 'But he hasn't been able to think of anything?'

Her mother gave her a sour look. 'The business is gone. And the bank is baying for its money.'

Lydie was having a hard time taking it all in. By the sound of it, things had been falling apart when she'd been home four months ago—but no one had seen fit to tell her. They had always had money! How could things have become so bad and she not know of it? She could perhaps understand her father keeping quiet; he was a very proud man. But—her mother? She was proud too, but...

'But where has all our money gone?' she asked. 'And why didn't Oliver...?'

'Well, naturally Oliver's business needed a little help.' Hilary Pearson bridled, just as if Lydie was laying some blame at her prized son's door. 'And why shouldn't your father invest heavily in him? You can't start a business from scratch and expect it to succeed in its first years. Besides, Madeline's family, the Ward-Watsons, are monied people. We couldn't let Oliver go around looking as though he hadn't a penny to his name!'

Which meant that he would take Madeline to only the very best restaurants and entertainment establishments, regardless of cost, Lydie realised. 'I didn't mean Oliver had—er—taken the money,' Lydie endeavoured to explain, knowing that her brother had started his own business five years ago and that, her father's firm doing well then, he had put up the money to set his son up in his own business. 'I meant why didn't Oliver say something to me?'

'If you cast your mind back, you'll recall that Oliver and Madeline were on holiday in South America the last time you were home. Poor Oliver works so hard; he needed that month's break.'

'His business is doing all right, is it?' Lydie enquired—and received another of her mother's sour looks for her trouble.

'As a matter of fact, he's decided to—um—cease trading.'

'You're saying that he's gone bust too?'

'Must you be so vulgar? Was all that expensive education lavished on you completely for nothing?' her mother grumbled. Though she did concede, 'All companies work on an overdraft basis—Oliver found it just too much of a struggle.

When he and Madeline come back from their honeymoon, Oliver will go and work in the Ward-Watson business.' She allowed herself the first smile Lydie had so far seen as she added, half to herself, 'I shouldn't be at all surprised if Oliver isn't made a director of the Ward-Watson conglomerate before he's much older.'

All of which was very pleasing, but this wasn't getting them anywhere. 'There won't be any money coming back to Dad from Oliver, I take it?'

'He'll need all the money he can lay his hands on to support his wife. Madeline *is* used to the finer things in life, you know.'

'Where's Dad now?' Lydie asked, her heart aching for the proud man who had always worked so hard. 'Is he down at the works?'

'Little point. Your father has already sold the works to pay off some debts—he's out of a job, and at his age nobody's going to employ him. Not that he would deign to work for anyone but himself.'

Oh, heavens, Lydie mused helplessly, it sounded as though things were even worse than she had started to imagine. 'Is he out in the grounds somewhere?'

'What grounds? Any spare ground has been sold. Not that, since it's arable land only, it made a lot.' And, starting to build up a fine head of steam, 'Apart from the house—which the bank wants a slice of, which means we have to leave— your father has sold everything else that he can. I've told him I'm not moving!' Her mother went vitriolically on in the same vein for another five minutes. Going on from talk of how they were on their beam-ends to state that if they had only a half of the amount the Ward-Watsons were forking out for their only daughter's fairy-tale wedding, the bank would be satisfied.

'Dad doesn't owe the bank very much, then?' Lydie asked, but before she could start to feel in any small way relieved, her mother was giving her a snappy reply.

'They're his one remaining creditor—he's managed to scrape enough together to pay off everybody else, plus most of his overdraft. But— today's Tuesday, and the bank say they have given him long enough. If they aren't in receipt of fifty thousand pounds by the end of banking on Friday—they move. And so do we! Can you imagine it? The disgrace? A fine thing it's going to look in Oliver's wedding announcement. Not ''Oliver Pearson of Beamhurst Court'', but ''Oliver Pearson of No Fixed Abode''. How shall we ever—?'

Her mother would have gone on, but Lydie interrupted. 'Fifty thousand doesn't sound such a fearfully large amount.'

'It does when you haven't got it. Nor any way of finding it either. Apart from the house, we're out of collateral. How can we borrow money with no way of repaying it? Nobody's going to loan us anything. Not that your father would ask in the circumstances. No, your father over-extended himself, the bank won't wait any longer—and now *I* have to pay!'

Lydie thought hard. 'The pictures!' she exclaimed after a moment. 'We could sell some of the family—'

'Haven't you been listening to a word I've said? Haven't I just finished telling you that everything, everything that isn't in trust for Oliver, has been sold? There's nothing left *to* sell. Nothing, absolutely nothing!'

Her mother looked closer to tears than Lydie had ever seen her, and suddenly her heart went out to her. For all her mother had never been the warmest mother in the world to her, Oliver being her pride and joy, Lydie loved her.

Lydie went impulsively over to her. 'I'm sorry,' she said gently, taking a seat next to her on the sofa. 'I'm so very sorry.' And, remembering her mother saying only a short while ago that it was time she paid something back for the expensive education she had received, 'What can I do?' she asked. While the amount of her inheritance was small, and nowhere near enough, Lydie was thinking in terms of asking to have that money released now and not two years hence, when she would attain the age of twenty-five, but her mother's reply shook her into speechlessness.

'You can go and see Jonah Marriott,' she said clearly. 'That's what you can do.'

Lydie stared at her, her green eyes huge. 'Jonah Marriott?' she managed faintly. She had only ever seen him once, and that was some seven years ago, but she had never forgotten the tall, good looking man.

'You remember him?'

'He came here one time. Didn't Dad lend him some money?'

'He did,' Hilary Pearson replied sharply. 'And now it's his turn to pay that money back.'

'He never repaid that money?' Lydie asked, feeling just a touch disappointed. He had seemed to her sixteen-year-old eyes such an honourable man—and she knew he had prospered greatly in the seven years that had elapsed.

'Coincidentally, the money he borrowed from your father is the same amount we need to stay on in this house.'

'Fifty thousand pounds?'

'Exactly the same. I can't impress on you enough that if the bank don't have their money by Friday, come Monday they'll be making representation to have us evicted. I'd go and see him myself, but when I mentioned it to your father he hit the roof and forbade me to do anything of the sort.'

Lydie could not imagine her mild-mannered father hitting the roof, especially to the wife he adored. But he must be under a tremendous amount of strain at the moment. No doubt he himself had previously asked Jonah Marriott to make some kind of payment off that loan. There was no way her father's pride would allow him to ask more than once. But to…

Her thoughts faded when just then the drawing room door opened and her father walked into the room. At least the man was tall, like her father, white-haired, like her father, but Lydie was shocked by the haggard look of him.

'Daddy!' she whispered involuntarily, and went hurriedly over to him. There was a dejected kind of slump to his shoulders which she found heart-breaking, and as she looked into his worn, tired face, she could not bear it. She put her arms round him and hugged him.

'What are you doing here?' he asked, putting her aside and sending her mother a suspicious look.

'I—thought I'd give Donna a chance to see how she'll cope without me,' Lydie invented, quickly hiding her shocked feelings. 'I'll give her a ring later. If she's okay I'll stay on, if that's all right with you?'

'Of course it's all right,' he replied with assumed joviality. 'This is your h...' He turned away and Lydie's heart ached afresh. She just knew he had been thinking that this was her home, but would not be for very much longer. 'Your mother been bringing you up to date with everything?' he enquired, his tone casual, but pride there, ready to be up in arms if his wife had breathed a word of his troubles.

'This wedding of Oliver's sounds a bit top-drawer. Are they going to have a marquee—you didn't finish telling me, Mother?'

Over the next half-hour Lydie observed at first hand the proud façade her father was putting up in front of her, and her heart went out to him. Looking at him, seeing the strain, the worry that seemed to be weighing him down, to go and see Jonah Marriott and ask him to repay the money he had borrowed from her father seven years ago did not seem such a hard task. Particularly as, if memory served, that money had only been loaned for a period of five years anyway.

'Your room's all ready for you.' Her mother took the conversation away from the wedding. 'If you want to go and freshen up,' she hinted.

'I've things to attend to in my study,' Wilmot Pearson commented before Lydie had answered. 'It's good to see you, Lydie. Let's hope you'll be able to stay.'

No sooner had he gone from the room than her mother was back to the forbidden subject. 'Well?' she questioned. 'Will you?'

Lydie knew what she was asking, just as she knew that she did not want to go and see Jonah Marriott. 'You're quite sure he hasn't paid that loan back?' she hedged. Her mother gave her a vinegary look. 'Perhaps he can't afford to pay it back,' Lydie commented. 'All firms work on an overdraft basis, you recently said so,' she reminded her mother, but, still shaken by the haggard look of her father, wondered why she was prevaricating about going to see Jonah Marriott.

Her mother chose to ignore her comments, instead scorning, 'Of course he can afford to pay it back—many times over. His father made a packet when he sold his department stores. Ambrose Marriott might be one tough operator but I can't see him giving to one son and not the other—and the younger Marriott boy hasn't done a day's work since the deal was done. They're all sitting on Easy Street,' her mother said with a heartfelt sigh, 'and just look at us!'

Lydie glanced at her parent, and while the last thing she wanted to do was to go and ask Jonah Marriott for the money he owed to her father, she knew that the time for prevaricating was over. She looked at her watch. Half past four. She had better get a move on. 'Do you have his number?'

'You can't discuss this with him over the telephone!' her mother snorted. 'You need to be there, face to face. You need to impress on him how—'

'I was going to ring his office for an appointment,' Lydie interrupted. 'He's hardly likely to see me without one.' And if he guesses what it's about he'll probably say no anyway!

'I don't want your father to catch you. You'd better make your call from your room,' Hilary Pearson decided. And, not allowing her daughter to consider changing her mind, 'I'll come up with you.'

'Marriott Electronics,' a pleasant voice answered when up in her old bedroom Lydie had dialled the number.

'Mr Marriott please,' Lydie said firmly, striving with all she had to keep her voice from shaking.

'Mr Jonah Marriott,' she tacked on, just in case Jonah had taken other members of the Marriott clan into the business.

'One moment, please,' the telephonist answered, but even though Lydie's stomach did a tiny somersault at the thought she might soon be speaking to the man she had seen only once but had never forgotten, she did not think she would be put through to him as easily as that.

Her stomach settled down when the next voice she heard was a calm and pleasant voice informing her, 'Mr Marriott's office.'

'Oh, hello,' Lydie said in a rush. 'My name's Lydie Pearson. I wonder if it's possible for me to have a word with Mr Marriott?'

'I'm afraid Mr Marriott's out of the office until Friday. Is there anything I can help you with?' Pleasant, polite, but Lydie knew she was getting nowhere.

'Oh,' she murmured, then paused for a moment, very much aware of her mother's tense gaze on her. 'I wanted to see him rather urgently. Um—perhaps I should ring him at home,' she pondered out loud, knowing in advance that she had small chance the woman—his PA, most probably—would let her have his private number.

'Actually, Mr Marriott is out of the country until late on Thursday evening.'

Oh, grief, she wanted this over and done with. 'I'll ring again on Friday,' Lydie said pleasantly, and rang off to be confronted by her mother, who wanted to hear syllable by syllable what had been said.

'We're going to lose the house!' Hilary Pearson cried. 'I know it! I know it!' And Lydie, who had never before seen her mother in a state of panic, began more than ever to appreciate how very dire the situation was—and she started to get angry—with Jonah Marriott.

'No, we won't,' she said as calmly as she could. 'I'll go and see Jonah Marriott on Friday, and I won't leave his office until I have the money he owes Dad.'

Lydie had no chance in the two days that followed to have second thoughts about going to see Jonah Marriott. With her father seeming to grow more drawn and careworn by the hour, not to mention her mother's endless insistence that Lydie was their only hope, Lydie knew that she had no choice but to go and see him.

Consequently, whenever the voice of reality would butt in to enquire what made her think anything she might say would make him promise to repay that money—he had let her father down; what difference did she think her appeal would make?—her emotions, her love for her parents and the calamity they were facing, would override the logic of her head.

Which in turn, over the days leading up to Friday, caused Lydie to grow angry again with Jonah Marriott. That anger turning to fury with him when she thought of how her father had lent him that money in good faith, and how Jonah had so badly let him down.

Her fury dimmed somewhat, though, whenever she recalled her only meeting with the man. She had occasionally helped her father in his study during her school holidays, and had known that someone was coming to the house in the hope of borrowing some money. It had gone from her mind that day, though, until she had come home and found him sitting in the drawing room of their home. She had been sixteen, a thin, lanky, terribly shy sixteen-year-old.

'Oh, I'm s-sorry,' she had stammered, blushing to the roots of her night-black hair. 'I didn't know anyone was in here!' He hadn't answered, but had done her the courtesy of rising to his feet. She had blushed again, but had felt obliged to ask, 'Are you waiting for Daddy?'

The man had superb blue eyes, quite a fantastic blue, she remembered thinking as he'd looked directly at her and commented in that wonderful all-male voice, 'If your daddy is Mr Wilmot Pearson, then, yes, I am.'

Her knees by that time were like so much jelly. But, at the same time, she could not help but think how ghastly it must be for him to have to come and ask to borrow some money, and, while she wanted to fly, she found she wanted more to make him feel better about it. 'I'm Lydie,' she stayed to tell him. 'Lydie Pearson.'

'Jonah Marriott,' he answered, and, treating her as a grown-up, his right hand came out.

Nervously, she shook hands with him, her colour a furious red as their hands met, his touch firm and warm. But still she could not leave him without trying to make him feel better. 'Would you like some tea, Mr Marriott?' she asked him shakily.

He had smiled then, and she had thought he had the most wonderful smile in the world. 'Thank you, no, Miss Pearson,' he had refused politely—and she had blushed again, this time at the dreadful thought that he was perhaps teasing her.

Just then, though, her father had come in. 'Sorry to keep you, Jonah. That phone call has settled most everything.' And, with a fond father's look to his daughter, 'You've met Lydie— soon to tear herself away from her beloved

Beamhurst and go back to school again after the summer break!'

'You'll miss her when she's gone, I'm sure,' Jonah answered with a glance to her, and Lydie had blushed again.

'I'll see you later,' she mumbled generally, and fled.

And so had begun a giant-sized crush on one Jonah Marriott. But she had not seen him later or ever again. That had not stopped her from finding out more about him. He had been in his late twenties then, and already had a thriving electronics business. From bits she had gleaned on separate occasions from her mother, from her father, and also from her brother Oliver, who at one time had gone around with a crowd that included Jonah's younger brother Rupert, she knew that Jonah was the elder son of Ambrose Marriott. Their father owned several department stores, and Jonah had felt obliged to go and work for his father. When Rupert had finished university, and had declared that there was nothing he would like better than to start work in the business, Jonah had felt free to leave the family business and start up his own company.

His father had not liked it, so Jonah had borrowed from the bank to get started. He had gone from success to success, but still owed the bank when he had wanted to expand his company. The banks had lent him as much as they could—it had not been enough. Too proud to ask his own father to lend him money—he had approached her father, a well-known businessman, instead.

The rest was history, Lydie fumed when, after a very fitful night's sleep, she awakened on Friday morning. Her father had lent Jonah Marriott fifty thousand pounds. Jonah Marriott, her idol for so long, had never paid him back. And Lydie was going to do something about it— this very day!

Had she experienced the smallest doubt about that, then that very small doubt evaporated into thin air when she went down to breakfast and saw that, while she had slept only fitfully, her father looked like a soul in torment and appeared not to have slept at all.

'And what are you going to do today?' he forced a cheerful note to ask. And she wished that she could tell him, Don't, Dad, I know all about it. But her father's pride was mammoth, and she could not take that away from him. Time enough for him to know when she came back from seeing Jonah Marriott and was able to tell him—if all went well—that Jonah would ring her father's bank and tell them, hopefully, that he would take on his debt.

'I haven't seen Aunt Alice in ages,' she answered, Aunt Alice being her mother's aunt, in
actual fact, and therefore Lydie's great-aunt. 'I
thought I might take a drive over to see her.'

'You're picking her up for the wedding next
week, aren't you?'

'She doesn't want to stay away from home
overnight.' Lydie tactfully rephrased part of what
her great-aunt had written in her last letter.

'We, your mother, Oliver and me, are going to
a hotel overnight, as you know. Your mother's
idea,' he muttered, but added dryly, 'Hilary will
be sorry her aunt won't be staying here.'

Lydie grinned. She thought Aunt Alice brilliant; her mother thought her a stubborn pain.
Lydie was not grinning after breakfast, though.
Dressed in a smart suit of powder blue, her dark
hair pulled back from her delicate features in a
classic knot, she got out her car ostensibly to
make the twenty mile drive to her aunt's home in
Penleigh Corbett in the next county.

While facing that she did not want to make the
journey to the London head office of Marriott
Electronics, since make it she must, she wanted
to be early. For all she knew she might have to
wait all day, but if Jonah Marriott was in the
building and refused to see her, then, since he had

to come out at some time, she was prepared to wait around to speak to him on his way out.

Her insides had been churned up ever since she had opened her eyes that morning, but the nearer she got to London, the more her churning insides were all over the place.

When the traffic started to snarl up she found a place to park her car and made it to the Marriott building by foot, tube and lastly taxi.

But once outside the building she experienced the greatest reluctance to go inside. For herself, perhaps having inherited her father's massive pride, she would have galloped in the opposite direction. Only this wasn't for her; it was for him.

Lydie had to do no more than recall her father's drawn look at breakfast and she was pushing through the plate-glass doors and heading for the reception desk.

The receptionist was busy dealing with one person and there was someone else waiting. 'Mr Marriott's PA is on her way down to see you.' The receptionist put down the phone to pass on the message to the suit-clad man she was dealing with.

Lydie closed her ears to the rest of it, her glance going over to where the lifts were. One started up and, from the changing numerals, she saw that the lift was making its way down from the top floor.

Without being fully aware of it, Lydie edged over to that lift. When the doors opened and a smart-looking woman of forty or so stepped out, and with a smile on her face went over to the man at the desk, Lydie stepped in and pressed the button for the top floor.

She knew she could quite well have got it wrong, but if her hunch was right, that had been Jonah Marriott's PA. If she had just come down from the top floor, then, to Lydie's mind, on the top floor was where she might find Jonah Marriott.

The lift stopped; she got out. She felt hot, sick, and knew that this was the worst thing she was ever going to have to do in her life. Instinct took her to the end of the carpeted corridor. With what intelligence her emotions had left her, it seemed to her that the man who was head of this corporation would have his office well away from the sound of the lift going up and down.

There were doors to offices on either side of the long corridor. Lydie ignored them and at the bottom of that corridor turned round a corner which opened out to show two doors blocking her way. Lydie hesitated, but only for a moment. She was by then starting to feel certain she had got it all wrong. Somehow, churned up, anxious, worried, she had got it all wrong, all muddled; she knew that she had. She went forward and, placing a hand on the handle to the door to the right, she paused for about half a second, then turned the handle.

Shock as the door swung inwards and she saw a man seated at a desk in front of her kept her speechless and motionless. He looked up, and as colour surged to her face so, his glance still on her face, he rose from his chair and began to come round his desk and over to her.

She was five feet nine inches tall, he looked down at her and—to her utter astonishment—commented, 'Still blushing, Lydie?' He remembered her, her blushes, from seven years ago?

'I'm L-Lydie Pearson,' she heard herself say inanely from somewhere far off.

'I know who you are,' he answered smoothly. 'Come in and take a seat,' he invited, and as she took a couple of steps into the room he closed the door behind her and touched a hand to her elbow.

In something of a daze she found she was seated on a chair some way to the side of his desk before she had got herself anywhere near of one piece.

'Haven't I changed at all in seven years?' she asked, her head still a little woolly that he had so instantly recognised her.

'I wouldn't say that,' Jonah replied pleasantly, his eyes flicking a glance over her still slender, but now curving deliciously in all the right places, shape. 'Elaine, my PA, made a note that a Lydie Pearson phoned last Tuesday. I recalled one black-haired, green-eyed Lydie Pearson with one hell of a superb complexion. It had to be you.' He paused, and then, while she was feeling a touch swamped that he thought she had a superb complexion, 'You're still Lydie Pearson?' he enquired.

Having thought she had her head more together, Lydie wasn't with him for a moment or two. 'Um…' she mumbled, then realised what he was asking. 'I'm not married,' she answered, and, with a quick glance to his ringless left hand, 'It doesn't look as if anybody's caught you either.'

His rather splendid mouth quirked upwards at the corners slightly. 'I have very long legs,' he confided.

'You sprint pretty fast at the word marriage?'

He did not answer. He didn't need to. 'So, how's the world treating you?' he asked.

Lydie looked away from his fantastic blue eyes and over to his laden desk. He had not been expecting this visit and from the look of his desk was extremely busy catching up on a backlog of work. Yet he seemed to have all the time in the world to idly converse with someone he barely knew, someone he had only ever clapped eyes on once—and that was seven years ago.

'Er—this isn't a social call,' Lydie stated abruptly.

'It isn't?' he questioned mildly—when she was sure he must *know* that it wasn't.

She experienced an unexpected urge to thump him that surprised her. She swallowed down that small burst of anger, but only when she felt marginally calmer was she able to coldly state, 'My father seems not to have fared as well, financially, over the last seven years as you yourself appear to have done.'

Jonah nodded, every bit as if he already knew that—and that annoyed her—before he coolly commented, 'That's what comes from constantly bailing out that brother of yours.'

How dared he blame Oliver? 'Oliver no longer has his own business!'

'That should make things easier for your father,' Jonah Marriott shot back at her, cool still.

Honestly! Again she wanted to hit him. 'My father's own business has gone too!' she retorted pithily, and saw that at last Jonah Marriott was taking her seriously.

'I'm very sorry to hear that. Wilmot is a first-class—'

'So you *should* be sorry!' she interrupted hotly. 'If you'd had the decency to honour that debt…'

'Honour that debt?' Jonah queried toughly, just as if he had not the first clue what she was talking about.

'You're trying to say that you have totally forgotten coming to my home seven years ago and borrowing fifty thousand pounds from my father?'

'I'm hardly likely to do that. If it wasn't for your father—'

'Then it's about time you paid that loan back!' she interrupted his flow hotly. And, suddenly too het-up to sit still, she jumped to her feet—to find Jonah Marriott was on his feet too, and was standing looking down on her. She saw him swiftly masking a look of surprise—at her nerve, no doubt. But she cared not if he thought she had an outrageous sauce to burst in on his busy morning without so much as a by your leave and demand the return of her father's money. Her father's peace of mind was at stake here. 'If my father doesn't have that fifty thousand pounds by the end of today's banking,' she hurtled on, 'we, that is my mother and father, will lose Beamhurst Court!'

'Lose...'

But Lydie was too angry to let him in. 'Beamhurst Court has been in my family for hundreds of years and my father has until only today to see that it stays in the family!' she charged on.

'You're exaggerating, surely?' Jonah Marriott managed to get in evenly, his eyes on her angry face, her sparking green eyes.

'I love Beamhurst! Does it look as if I'm exaggerating?' she erupted. But calmed down a little to concur, 'It's true my father invested heavily in Oliver's company, but my father didn't know his own firm was going to suffer a downturn.'

'So he borrowed as much as he could from the banks, putting Beamhurst Court up as collateral,' Jonah took up. 'And when your brother's firm went belly-up, and your father settled his son's creditors, there was nothing left in the kitty to settle his own debts.'

'You know this?' she asked, starting to feel her anger on the rise again that he should be aware of the situation and still refuse to repay her father.

'I didn't,' Jonah replied, defusing her anger somewhat. 'From what you've said, that seems the most likely way it went.' And disconcertingly he asked, 'And what's your brother doing in all of this?'

Lydie did not care for his question. It weakened her argument. Her father was distraught—while Oliver did nothing. 'He… I haven't seen Oliver. I only came home on Tuesday,' she excused, and defended her elder brother. 'Oliver's getting married a week tomorrow. There's a lot to arrange. He's staying with his fiancée's people to help with any last-minute problems they…' Her voice trailed away.

'Let's hope he makes a better job of it than he made of his business,' Jonah commented, but, before she could take exception, 'Big do, is it?'

Lydie could have done without that remark too. In the instance of her family being on their uppers—and she was coming to realise more and more that her father constantly financing her brother's business was largely responsible for that—it did seem a bit over the top to have such a pomp of a wedding.

'The bride's parents are paying for everything,' she felt obligated to admit, her pride taking something of a hammering here. 'Look, we're getting away from the point!' she said snappily. 'You owe my father money. Money he needs, *now*, if he is to remain in the only home he has ever known, the home he loves.'

'Fifty thousand pounds will assure that?' Jonah asked, doubting it.

'My father has sold everything he can possibly sell in order to meet his debts. All that remains is an overdraft of fifty thousand pounds at the bank that he knows, and they know, he cannot find—nor has any likelihood of finding. They have given him until today to try to find that money anyway. He cannot,' she ended, and her voice started to fracture. 'A-and he looks t-terrible.'

Abruptly she turned away from Jonah, knowing that her emotions as she thought of her dear distracted father had brought her close to tears. She went to stare unseeing out of the window and swallowed hard as she fought for control. Her pride would never survive if she broke down in front of this hard man.

When she felt she had control she turned towards the door, knowing instinctively that she had pleaded her father's cause in vain. It had been a long shot anyway, she realised. Had Jonah Marriott the smallest intention of repaying that money, he would have done so long before this.

She took a step to the door—but was halted when Jonah, having not moved from where she had left him, stated, 'Obviously your father doesn't know you've come here.'

Lydie turned. 'He's a proud man,' she replied with a tilt of her head.

'His daughter's pretty much the same,' Jonah said quietly, his eyes on her proud beauty.

She wished she could agree. Albeit she had not come to the Marriott building for herself, she had not been too proud to come here today—even if that money was still owing. 'Should you ever bump into my father, I'd be obliged if you did not tell him I came here,' she requested coldly.

For answer Jonah Marriott went round to his desk. 'I won't—but I think he'll know,' he drawled, to her alarm. And, even while she was instantly ready to go for Jonah Marriott's jugular, he was opening a drawer in his desk, taking out a chequebook, and asking, 'Who do you want the cheque made out to, Lydie?'

'Y-you'll pay?' she asked, shaken rigid, but in no mind to refuse—no matter how little he offered. He did not answer but picked up his pen. She went over to stand at the other side of his desk. 'My father. Would you make it out to my father, please?' she said quickly, before he could change his mind.

It was done. In next to no time the cheque was written and Jonah was handing it to her across the desk. Hardly daring to breathe, lest this be some sort of evil game he was playing, Lydie inspected the cheque. It was made out to Wilmot Pearson. The date was right. The cheque was signed. But the amount was wrong. Jonah had made it out for fifty-five thousand pounds!

'Fifty-*five* thousand...?'

'The bank will be adding interest—daily, I don't doubt. Call it interest on the debt.'

He meant his debt, of course. Feeling stunned, then beginning to feel little short of elated, Lydie looked up and across at him. She was about to thank him when she looked at the cheque again and noticed that it was not a company cheque, as she would have thought, but a personal cheque— and a large chunk of her elation fell away. Anybody could write a personal cheque for fifty-five thousand pounds, but that did not necessarily mean there was any money in that bank account. Was this some kind of sick joke Jonah Marriott was playing, to pay her back for her impertinence in daring to walk unannounced into his office and demand he paid what he owed?

'There's money in this account to meet this amount?' she questioned.

'Not yet,' he admitted. Though, before her last ray of hope should disappear, 'But there will be...' he paused '...by the time you get to your father's bank.'

'You're—sure?' she asked hesitantly.

Jonah Marriott eyed her steadily. 'Trust me, Lydie,' he said quietly—and, strangely, she did.

'Thank you,' she said, and held out her right hand.

'Goodbye,' he said, and, with that wonderful smile she had remembered all these years, 'Let's hope it's not another seven years before we meet again.'

She smiled too, and could still feel the warm firm pressure of his right hand on hers as she waltzed out of the Marriott building and into the street. She remembered his blue eyes and...

She pushed him from her mind and concentrated on what to do first. She had half a notion to ring her mother and tell her the outcome of her visit to Jonah Marriott. Lydie then thought of the cheque that was burning a hole in her bag. She had been going to take it straight to her father, to tell him everything was all right now. To tell him that Jonah Marriott had paid in full, with interest, the money he had owed him for so long. But, with Jonah saying that the funds would be there by the time she got to her father's bank—presumably all that was needed was for Jonah to pick up a phone and give his instructions—would it not be far better for her to bank the money now and tell her father afterwards?

Lydie decided there and then—thanking Jonah for the suggestion—that she would bank the money before she went home. Yes, that was much the better idea. As things stood she had plenty of time to get home, hand the cheque over to her father and for him to take the cheque personally to his bank. But who knew what traffic hold-ups there might be on the road. Much better—thank you, Jonah—to bank the cheque first and then go home.

Having found a branch of the bank which her father used, it was a small matter to have her father's account located, the money paid in, and to receive the bank's receipt in return.

Oh, Jonah. Her head said she should be cross with him for his tardiness in paying what was owed. But she couldn't be cross. In fact, on that drive back to Beamhurst Court, she was hard put to it not to smile the whole time.

The house was secure and, although with not so much land as they had once owned, it was still in the hands of the Pearsons. While her father was unlikely to start in business on his own account again, he no longer, as Jonah had put it, needed to bail her brother out ever again either. Her mother had hinted that her father had been looking into the possibility of some consultancy work.

Surely all his years of expertise were not to be wasted.

Optimistically certain that everything would be all right from now on, Lydie drew up outside the home she so loved and almost danced inside as she went looking for her parents. Had today turned out well or hadn't it? She understood now why, when she'd asked Jonah not to tell her father she had been to see him, Jonah had replied, 'I won't—but I think he'll know.' Of course her father would know. The minute she told her proud father that his overdraft was cleared he would want to know where the money had come from. Jonah would not have to tell her father—she would. She could hardly wait to see his joy.

'Here you both are!' she said on opening the drawing room door and seeing her parents there— her father looking a shadow of his former self.

Her mother gave her a quick expectant look, but it was her father who asked, 'How was your great-aunt Alice?'

'Actually, Dad, I lied,' Lydie confessed. 'I haven't been to see Aunt Alice.'

He gave her a severe look. 'For someone who has lied to her father you're looking tremendously pleased with yourself,' he remarked. 'I trust it was a lie for the good of mankind?'

'Not exactly,' she replied, and quickly opening her bag she took out the receipt for the money she had paid into his bank account. 'I went to see Jonah Marriott.'

'You went—to see Jonah Marriott?' he asked in surprise. He took the folded receipt she held out, opened it out, read the very little that was written there, but which meant so much, and—his face darkened ominously. 'What *is* this?' he demanded, as though unable to believe that an amount of fifty-five thousand pounds had been paid into his account.

'Your overdraft is cleared, Dad.' She explained that which he seemed to have difficulty in taking in.

'Cleared!' he echoed, it passing him by completely just then that she knew about his financial problems, and his tone of voice such that, had she not known better, Lydie would have thought it was the calm before the storm.

'I went to see Jonah Marriott, as I said. He gave me a cheque for the money he owed you. I paid it into your bank on my—' She didn't get to finish.

'You did *what*?' her father roared, and Lydie stared at him in astonishment. Her mild-mannered father *never* roared!

'You n-needed the money,' she mumbled anxiously—this wasn't at all how she had imagined it. 'Jonah Marriott owed you fifty thousand pounds—I went and asked him for it. He added five…'

'You went and *asked* him for fifty thousand pounds?' her father shouted. 'Have you *no* pride?'

'He owed it to you. He…'

'He did *not,*' her father cut her off furiously.

'He—didn't?' Lydie gasped, looking over to her mother, who had told her that he did, but who was now more interested in looking at the curtains than in meeting her eyes.

'He does not owe me anything!' her father bellowed. 'Not a penny!' Lydie flinched as she turned her head to stare uncomprehendingly at the man who, prior to that moment, had never raised his voice to her in his life. 'Oh, what have you done, Lydie?' he asked, suddenly defeated, and she felt then that she would rather he shouted at her than that he should sound so utterly beaten. 'Any money Jonah Marriott borrowed from me was paid back, with good interest, more than three years ago.'

CHAPTER TWO

'HE PAID you back!' Lydie gasped. And, reeling from what her father had just revealed, 'But Mother said—' Lydie broke off, her stricken gaze going from her mortified father to her mother.

This time her mother did meet her eyes, defiantly. But it was Wilmot Pearson who found his voice first, and, transferring his look to his wife, 'What did you tell her?' he demanded angrily.

'Somebody had to do something!' she returned hostilely, entirely unrepentant.

'But you knew Jonah Marriott had repaid that loan—repaid it ahead of time. I told you. I clearly remember telling—'

'*Mother!* You *knew*?' Lydie chipped in, horrified. 'You knew all the time that that money had been repaid—yet you let me go and ask Jonah for money!' Oh, how she had asked him. No, Please will you lend us some money? but 'This isn't a social call' she had told him shortly, and had gone from there to suggest he didn't have any decency and that it was about time he paid that loan back—when all the time he already had. And she

47

had thought he looked a bit surprised! No wonder! 'Mother, how could you?'

Her mother did not care to be taken to task, and was at her arrogant worst when she retorted, 'Far better to owe Jonah Marriott money than the bank. At least this way we get to keep the house.'

'Don't be so sure about that!' Wilmot Pearson chipped in heavily—and uproar broke out between her parents for several minutes; he determined he would sell the house to pay Jonah Marriott and her mother said her father would be living elsewhere on his own if he did, and that Beamhurst was to be preserved to be passed down to Oliver. It was painful to Lydie to hear them, but when her mother, retorting that at least they wouldn't be opening the doors to the bailiffs come Monday morning, seemed to be getting the better of the argument, her father turned and vented his frustration out on his daughter.

'He—Jonah—he gave you a cheque, just like that, did he? You told him you wanted that "loan" I made him back—and he paid up without a murmur?'

'He—um—said he had never forgotten how you helped him out that time. He was grateful to you, I think,' Lydie answered, starting to wish that her mother had never phoned her last Tuesday.

'So he gave you fifty-five thousand pounds out of gratitude and without a word that he had already settled that debt? How the devil do you suppose I'm going to pay him back?' her father exploded, and in high temper, 'Why *ever* didn't you bring that cheque home to *me first*?' he demanded. 'Why in the world did you *bank it* without first consulting me?'

Lydie felt she would have brought the cheque to her father, had not Jonah Marriott put the idea of banking it first into her head. And suddenly she began to get the feeling that, one way and another, she had been well and truly manipulated here. First by her mother, very definitely by her mother, and secondly by Jonah Marriott himself.

'Well?' Her father interrupted her thoughts.

'It seemed the best way to do it,' she answered lamely. 'If there had been any sort of a traffic snarl-up I could have been too late for the bank here. And I knew—' thank you, Mother '—that the bank wanted their money by today.'

'And they've got it—and it's for certain they'll hang on to it!' he stated agitatedly. 'There's absolutely no chance they'll let me have it back again.' He sighed heavily. 'I'd better go and see Jonah.'

'I'll go!' Lydie said straight away, as she knew she must.

'*You,*' her father erupted, 'have done enough!
You can stay here with your mother and dream
up your next scheme.'

That comment was extremely unfair, in Lydie's
opinion, but she understood his pride must be
hurting like the very devil. 'Please let me go?'
she pleaded. He hesitated for the merest moment,
and Lydie rushed on quickly, 'You're not the only
one with any pride,' she added—and all at once
her father seemed to fold.

He looked at her, his normally quite reserved
daughter who, up until then, had caused him very
little grief. 'None of this has been very easy for
you either, has it?' he queried, more in the calm
tone she was familiar with. And, relenting, if reluctantly, 'We'll go and see him together,' he
conceded.

That wasn't what Lydie wanted either. 'I'll go
and ring him,' she offered.

'Not go and see him?'

'I'll probably have to make an appointment
first.' In this instance of eating extra-large por-
tions of humble pie, it seemed more diplomatic
to try and get an appointment first rather than to
go barging straight into his office.

'We'll make the call from my study,' Wilmot
Pearson declared, and, giving his wife a frosty
look in passing, for which, since her home was

for the moment secure, she cared not a jot, he and
Lydie went from the drawing room and to his
study.

She was glad that her father allowed her to
make the call and did not insist on doing that
himself, but her insides were on the churn again
as she dialled the Marriott Electronics number.

Again when she asked to speak with Mr Jonah
Marriott she was put through to his PA. 'Hello,
it's Lydie Pearson…'

'Oh, good afternoon,' the PA answered pleasantly, before Lydie could continue. 'I missed seeing you this morning.' And Lydie realised that
plainly Jonah must have made some comment to
his PA about her visit—probably something along
the lines of Don't ever let that woman come in
here again—she's too expensive. Lydie hoped he
hadn't revealed the full content of her visit to his
confidential assistant. 'I'm afraid Mr Marrriott's
at a meeting. If you would like to leave a message?'

Blocked. 'I should like to see him some time.
Later this afternoon if that's possible.'

'He's flying to Paris tonight, but…'

Something akin to jealousy gave Lydie a small
thump at the thought that he would be dallying
the weekend in Paris. Ridiculous, she scoffed. But
she began to realise she had inherited a little of

her mother's arrogance in that she would beg for nothing. 'I'll give him a call next week. It's not important,' Lydie butted in pleasantly, wished the PA an affable goodbye, and turned to relay the conversation to her waiting father. 'Try not to worry, Dad,' she added quietly. Having been set up by her mother, she was not feeling all that friendly towards her, but attempted anyway to make things better between her parents. 'And try not to be too cross with Mother; she only did what she did to help.'

Wilmot Pearson looked as if he might have a lot to say about that, but settled for a mild, 'I know.'

The atmosphere in the house was not good for the rest of the day, however, and Lydie took herself off for a walk with a very great deal on her mind. She still felt crimson around the ears when she thought of the way she had gone to Jonah Marriott's office and demanded fifty thousand pounds!

Oh, heavens! But—why on earth had he given it to her? Not only that, but he had made sure his cheque was banked and not returned to him with a polite note from her father. 'There's money in this account to meet this amount?' she had asked him. 'There will be…by the time you get to your father's bank,' he had said, as in Make haste and get there—and she had fallen for it!

Lydie carried on walking, not knowing where she was emotionally. With that money in the bank her father had some respite from his worries—and he sorely needed that respite. Against that, though, since it was she who had asked for, and taken, that money, regardless of where she had deposited it, she was beginning to realise that the debt was not her father's but hers; solely hers.

Feeling quite sick as she accepted that realisation, all she could do was to wonder where in creation she was going to find fifty-five thousand pounds with which to repay him? That question haunted her for the remainder of her walk.

She returned home knowing that adding together the second-hand value of her car, the pearls her parents had given her for her twenty-first birthday and her small inheritance—if she could get into it—she would be lucky if she was able to raise as much as ten thousand pounds!

She went to bed that night knowing that Jonah Marriott's hope that it would not be another seven years before they met again must have been said tongue in cheek. He must have known she would be on the phone wanting to see him the moment she discovered his loan from her father had been repaid long since. Jonah Marriott, without a doubt, had told his PA to inform her when she rang that he could not see her.

Why he would do that, Lydie wasn't very sure, and conceded that very probably he'd given his PA no such instruction. It was just one Lydie Pearson feeling very much out of sorts where he was concerned. Him and his 'Obviously your father doesn't know you've come here.' It was *obvious* to her, *now*, that Jonah knew her father would have soon stopped her visit had he the merest inkling of what she was doing.

Lydie spent a wakeful night with J. Marriott Esquire occupying too much space in her head for comfort. Over-sexed swine! She hoped he was enjoying himself in Paris—whoever she was.

The atmosphere in her home was no better when she went down to breakfast on Saturday morning. Lydie saw a whole day of monosyllabic conversation and of watching frosty glances go back and forth.

'I think I'll go and see Aunt Alice. Truthfully,' she added at her father's sharp look.

'While you're there for goodness' sake check what she intends to wear to the wedding next Saturday,' her mother instructed peevishly. 'She's just as likely to turn up in that disgraceful old gardening hat and wellingtons!'

Lydie was glad to escape the house, and drove to Penleigh Corbett and the small semi-detached house which her mother's aunt, to her mother's embarrassment, rented from the local council.

To Lydie's dismay, though, the sprightly eighty-four-year-old was looking much less sprightly than when she had last seen her, for all she beamed a welcome. 'Come in, come in!' she cried. 'I didn't expect to see you before next week.'

They were drinking coffee fifteen minutes later when, feeling quite perturbed by her great-aunt's pallor, Lydie enquired casually, 'Do you see your doctor at all?'

'Dr Stokes? She's always popping in.'

'What for?' Lydie asked in alarm.

'Nothing in particular. She just likes my chocolate cake.'

Lydie had to stamp down hard on her need to know more than that. Great-Aunt Alice was anti people discussing their ailments. 'Are you taking any medication?' Lydie asked tentatively.

'Do you know anybody over eighty who isn't?' Alice Gough bounced back. 'How's your mother? Has she come to terms yet with the fact dear Oliver wants to take a wife?'

'You're wicked,' Lydie accused.

'Only the good die young,' Alice Gough chuckled, and took Lydie on a tour of her garden. They had lunch of bread, cheese and tomatoes, though Lydie observed that the elderly lady ate very little.

Lydie visited with her great-aunt for some while, then, thinking she was probably wanting her afternoon nap, said she would make tracks back to Beamhurst Court. 'Come back with me!' she said on impulse—her mother would kill her. 'You could stay until after the wedding, and—'

'Your mother would love that!'

'Oh, do come,' Lydie appealed.

'I've got too much to do here,' Alice Gough refused stubbornly.

'You don't—' Lydie broke off. She had been going to say You don't look well. She changed it to, 'You're a little pale, Aunty. Are you sure you're all right?'

'At my age I'm entitled to creak a bit!' And with that Lydie had to be satisfied.

'I'll come over early next Saturday,' she said as her great-aunt came out to her car with her.

'Tell your mother I'll leave my gardening gloves at home,' Alice Gough answered completely po-faced.

Lydie had to laugh. 'Wicked, did I say?' And she drove away.

The nearer she got to Beamhurst Court, though, the more her spirits started to dip. She was worried about her great-aunt, she was worried about the cold war escalating between her parents, and she was worried, quite desperately worried, about where in the world she was going to find fifty-five thousand pounds with which to pay Jonah Marriott.

And, having thought about him—not that he and that wretched money were ever very far from the front of her mind—she could not stop thinking about him—in Paris. She hoped it kept fine for him. That made her laugh at herself—she was getting as sour as her mother.

'Aunty doesn't look so well,' Lydie reported to her mother.

'What's the matter with her?'

'She didn't say, but...'

'She wouldn't! Typical!' Hilary Pearson sniffed. 'Some man called Charles Hillier has been on the phone for you.'

'Charlie. He's Donna's brother. Did he say why he phoned?'

'I told him to ring back.'

Poor Charlie; he was as shy as she had been one time. But while to a large extent she had grown out of her shyness, Charlie never had. He had probably been terrified of her mother. Lydie went up to her room and dialled his number. 'I'm sorry I was out when you rang,' she apologised. She was very fond of Charlie. He was never going to set her world on fire, but she thought of him as a close friend.

'Did I ring your mother at a bad time?' he asked nervously.

'No—she's a little busy. My brother's getting married next Saturday.' Lydie covered the likelihood that her mother had been rude to Charlie if he had been in stammering mode.

'Ah. Right,' he said, and went on to say he had planned to ask her to go to the theatre with him tonight, and had been shaken when he'd rung Donna to hear that she had already left Donna's home. 'You're helping with the wedding, I expect,' he went on. 'Would you have any free time? I've got the tickets and everything. I thought we'd have a meal afterwards and you could stay the night here, if you like. That is… You've probably got something else arranged?' he ended diffidently.

'I'd love to go to the theatre with you,' Lydie accepted. 'Would it put you out if I stayed?'

'Your bed's already made up,' he said happily back, and she could almost see his face beaming.

Lydie went to tell her mother that she was going to the theatre with Charlie Hillier and would not be back until mid-morning the next day.

'You're spending the night with him?'

'He has a flat in London. It could be quite late when we finish. It seems more sensible to stay than to drive home afterwards.'

'You're having an affair with him?' her mother shook her by accusing.

'Mother!' Honestly! Charlie wouldn't know how to go about an affair. Come to think of it, Lydie mused whimsically, neither would she. 'Charlie's just a friend. More like a brother than anything. And nothing more than that.'

Lydie went back upstairs and put a few things into an overnight bag. Charlie had overcome his shyness one time to attempt to kiss her, but had confessed, when they'd both ended up mightily embarrassed, that he had kissed her more because he thought he ought to than anything else. From then on a few ground rules had been established and they had progressed to be good friends who, on the odd, purely spontaneous moment, would sometimes kiss cheeks in greeting or parting. She had stayed at his flat several times with Donna and young Thomas before baby Sofia had come along. But over the last year Lydie had a couple of times comfortably spent the night in his spare bedroom after a late night in London.

The play Charlie took her to was a light-hearted, enjoyable affair. 'Shall we get a drink?' he asked at interval time.

For herself, she wasn't bothered, but felt that Charlie probably wanted one. 'A gin and tonic sounds a good idea,' she accepted, and went with him to mingle with the crowd making their slow way to the bar.

They eventually entered the bar, where she decided to wait to one side while Charlie got the drinks. But Lydie had taken only a step or two when all of a sudden, with her heart giving the oddest little flip, she came face to face with none other than Jonah Marriott!

He stopped dead, his wonderful blue eyes on the riot of colour that flared to her face. 'I thought you were in Paris!' she blurted out, surprised at seeing him so unexpectedly causing the words to rush from her before she could stop them.

'I came back,' he replied smoothly.

She could do without his smart remarks. It was obvious he had come back! 'I need to see you,' she said tautly—by no chance did she intend to discuss her business where they stood. But suddenly she spotted something akin to devilment in his eyes and knew then that if he answered with something smart—That's what they all say—she was going to hit him, regardless of where they were.

He did not say what she expected, but instead drawled, 'Monday, same time, same place,' and they both moved on.

She felt unnerved, unsettled, and wished it were Monday, when she would march into his office and demand to know why he had given her a cheque for fifty-five thousand pounds! She was glad when Charlie returned with their drinks.

But Lydie started to feel worse than ever when she abruptly realised that to demand why of Jonah wasn't relevant. What was relevant was to make some arrangement with him to pay him back. Her spirits sank—how? With that question unanswered, she flicked a glance around—her gaze halting when she spotted Jonah. He was not looking at her but over in their direction, at the tall manly back of her dark-haired escort. Her glance slid from Jonah to the stunning, last word in perfection blonde he was escorting. And she'd thought her spirits couldn't get any lower!

Not wanting Jonah to catch her looking in his direction, Lydie tore her eyes away from the sophisticated blonde. 'How's business?' she asked Charlie.

'We've got a new woman at the office—she started a couple of weeks ago,' he said, and went red.

'Charlie Hillier!' Lydie teased. 'You're smitten.'

He laughed self-consciously, and she smiled affectionately at him. 'Well, she is rather nice.'

'Are you going to ask her out?'

He looked horrified. 'Heck, no! I hardly know her!'

Dear Charlie. He had been a frequent visitor to his sister's home, but Lydie had known him a year before they had begun to graduate from more than an exchanged hello and goodbye.

She did not see Jonah again that night, and had a late supper with Charlie and went to bed. They shared toast and eggs for breakfast, and Lydie drove home to Beamhurst Court with her head on the fidget with thoughts of her great-aunt, her parents and a man who appeared to enjoy escorting sophisticated blondes to the theatre. Had he taken the blonde with him to Paris?

She awoke on Monday in a state of anxiety. 'Couldn't sleep?' her father asked when she went down to an early breakfast.

She didn't know about couldn't sleep—he did not look as if he had slept at all! She looked at his weary face and knew she should tell him that she was going to see Jonah Marriott, but somehow she could not. 'I thought, with Mother wanting Aunt Alice to look smart on Saturday, that I'd better make an effort and get myself a new outfit,' Lydie announced. And, seeing that her father looked about to remind her of a very important phone call they had to make, 'I thought,' she hurried on, 'that while I'm in London I'd call in at the Marriott building and make an appointment for us to see Jonah. He was abroad somewhere last week, so I suppose he's still got a lot of catching up to do and will be too busy to see me today.' She was lying to her father again, and hated doing so, but this, seeing Jonah, she felt most strongly, was something she had to do on her own.

But her father was nobody's fool. 'How did you manage to get an appointment with him last Friday? He would have been catching up then too.'

'On Friday I thought he owed you money. I didn't bother to make an appointment. I just sort of barged my way in.

Her father looked appalled. 'You...' he began.

'Please, Dad,' she butted in. 'I was wrong. I know it. Which is why I feel I have to do it the right way this time.'

'I can ring from here. He...'

'I know I've embarrassed you by going to see him at all. But please try to understand—I need to be involved here. I can't let you take over from me.'

Her father grunted. But, muttering something about being determined to see Jonah at the first possible opportunity, he agreed to allow her to make the appointment.

Lydie was walking into the Marriott Electronics head office building when she started to half wish her father was with her. She felt sick, shaky, and she heartily wished this imminent interview were all over and done with.

She rode up in the same lift, walked shakily along the same corridor and turned round the corner without an earthly idea of what she would say to the man. Eating humble pie did not come easy.

Outside his door, she paused to take a deep breath. She knew she was ten minutes earlier than she had been on Friday, but she was too wound up to wait for ten minutes of torturous seconds to tick by.

She put her right hand on the door handle and took a deep breath, and then, tilting her chin a proud fraction, she turned the handle and with her heart pounding went in.

Jonah Marriott was not alone, but was mid-instruction to the woman Lydie had seen step out of the lift last Friday. He looked up and got to his feet to greet her. 'Lydie,' he said and, turning to his PA, introduced them to each other.

'We've spoken on the phone,' Elaine Edwards commented with a smile, and obviously aware of this appointment, even if Lydie was early for it, she picked up her papers, said, 'I'll come back later,' and went through into her own office and closed the door.

'Enjoy the play?' Jonah asked, taking Lydie out of her stride—she had intended to pitch straight in there with some ''The debt is mine but I can't pay''-type dialogue.

'Very much,' she answered, with barely an idea just then what the play had been about.

'Take a seat,' he offered. 'Was that your steady boyfriend?'

'Er—what? No. Um—I see him sometimes,' she replied, wondering what that had got to do with anything, though she would not have minded asking if the blonde were his steady. Not that she was terribly interested, of course.

She took the seat he indicated and opened her mouth, ready to put this conversation along the lines it was to go, when, 'Coffee?' he asked, and she knew then that she was not the one in charge of how the conversation went—he was. He was playing with her!

'No, thank you,' she refused, her tone perhaps a little less civil than it should be in the circumstances. 'When I came here last Friday I was under the impression you had not honoured the debt you owed my father. I…'

'So I gathered,' Jonah replied, having retaken his seat behind his desk, leaning back to study her.

She did not care to be studied; it rattled her. 'You should have told me!' she flared. 'You *knew* you had repaid that loan!

He smiled—it was a phoney smile. 'I knew I would end up getting the blame.'

Just then guilt, embarrassment, and every other emotion she had experienced since seeing him again last Friday after seven years, all rose up inside her, causing her control to fracture. 'And so you should!' she snapped. 'You set me up!' she accused hotly.

The phoney smile abruptly disappeared. He cared not for her tone; she could tell. '*I* set you up?' he challenged. 'My memory is usually so good, but correct me if I'm wrong—did I ask you to come here, dunning me for money?'

Dunning! Put like that it sounded awful. Her fury all at once fizzled out. 'I *trusted* you,' she said quietly. 'Yet you, the way you hinted that I should pay the cheque into my father's bank straight away, made sure I did just that.'

Jonah Marriott eyed her uncompromisingly. 'Would you rather I had not given you that cheque?' he questioned toughly. 'Would you prefer that your father was still in hock to his bank?'

She blanched. It was becoming more and more clear to her that Jonah Marriott was much too smart for her. He knew, as she had just accepted, that by taking the money from him she had allowed her father some respite. At least there wasn't a ''For Sale'' notice being posted in their grounds that morning. 'Why did you give me that money?' she asked. 'And why make it pretty certain that I'd bank it first and tell my father afterwards?'

Jonah shrugged. 'Seven years ago your father's faith in me, his generosity, made it possible for me to successfully carry out my ideas. From what you told me on Friday, Wilmot was in a desperate fix with no way out. Without a hope of repaying any financial assistance, I knew there was no way he would accept my help.'

That was true. Lydie sighed. She felt defeated suddenly. 'My father wanted to see you as soon as possible. I said, since I was coming to London today, that I'd make an appointment and that we would both come and see you.'

Jonah eyed her solemnly. 'You lied to him?'

'I'm not proud of it. Until last week, when I told him I was going to see a great-aunt but came here instead, I had never lied to my father in my life.'

Jonah nodded. 'I can see reason for you lying to him about coming here the first time—obviously either your brother or your mother has been bending your ear with falsehoods too—but why lie to your father about coming here today?'

'Because—because he's been a very worried man for long enough. It's time somebody else in the family took some of the load.'

'Namely you?'

'It was I who asked you for that money. I who—er—um—borrowed it, not him. The debt is mine.'

Jonah stared at her for some long moments. 'It's yours?' he queried finally.

'My father didn't ask for the money. Nor would he. As you so rightly said, he wouldn't—not for something he couldn't see his way to pay back.' She broke off and looked into a pair of fantastic blue eyes that now seemed more academically interested than annoyed. 'The debt is mine,' she resumed firmly, 'and no one else's. I've come today to...' her firm tone began to slip '...t-to try and make arrangements to repay you.'

He looked a tinge surprised. 'You have money?' he enquired nicely.

Lydie swallowed down a sudden spurt of ire. Was she likely to have taken money from him had she money of her own? 'I intend to sell my car and my pearls, and there's a small inheritance due in a couple of years that I may be able to get my hands on—but otherwise I have only what I earn.'

'You're working?' he enquired.

He was unnerving her. 'I'm between jobs at the moment,' she answered shortly. 'I was leaving my job this week anyway, but left early when my mother telephoned last Tuesday and—' Lydie broke off and could have groaned out loud. Jonah Marriott was a clever man. From what she had just said he would easily deduce it had been her mother who had told her that he had reneged on his debt to her father.

Jonah did not refer to it, however, but asked instead, 'What sort of work do you normally do?'

'I'm a nanny. I look after children.'

'You enjoy it?'

'Very much. I thought, once Oliver's wedding is out of the way, that I'd look around for something else.'

'In the same line?'

Lydie gave him a slightly exasperated look, and was wondering what his questioning had got to do with her repaying him when it all at once dawned on her it had *everything* to do with it. She was proposing to pay him back fifty-five thousand pounds—out of her earnings. 'Actually—it, the job—it pays quite well,' she offered—rather feebly, she had to admit.

He smiled again, that smile she had no faith in. 'Even so, I don't know that I want to wait thirty years for you to save up.'

'You can't put the debt at my father's door!' she erupted fiercely, her lovely green eyes at once sparking fire.

He stared at her, unsmiling, for several long moments. 'I have no intention of doing that,' he stated.

'You accept that the debt is mine, and mine alone?'

'You're determined to take the—er—debt on as your own?'

She did not have to think twice about it when she thought of her poor dear father's haggard face, his shoulders bent with worry. 'I am,' she said. 'I'll make arrangements to…'

'You have a plan?'

'No,' she had to confess. 'But I…'

'Don't go selling your car or your jewellery,' Jonah advised, it seeming plain to him, evidently, that she hadn't any idea how to meet her debt.

'I don't know how else to begin to make a start on repaying you.'

Jonah leaned back, studying her as if he liked what he saw. 'Perhaps I can come up with something,' he remarked.

It was her turn to stare at him. 'You'll—think of something?' she queried eagerly.

He afforded her a pleasant look. 'Leave it with me.'

Leave it with him? That was much too vague! She'd been fretting about it all over the weekend. She needed this sorted out now. 'You've no idea now?'

'I'll need to think about it.'

'When will you let me know?' The sooner they had matters arranged, the sooner she could make future plans—perhaps she could find work on her time off. Anything extra would be welcome, the sooner to pay off that colossal debt. 'If you could tell me this week some time?' she hinted. 'I'd—'

'Let's see,' he cut in pleasantly. 'Today's Monday—I should have some idea by, say, Saturday.'

'You'll tell me on Saturday?' she asked urgently. Then remembered, and cried, 'Oh—I'll be at Oliver's wedding on Saturday!'

That smile she didn't trust a bit was in evidence again. 'I'll see you there,' he informed her.

'You're going to…? You've had an invitation?'

'I'm sure you'll remedy that oversight,' Jonah Marriott answered coolly.

Lydie stared at him in disbelief. 'You want to go to Oliver's wedding?' Why, for goodness' sake, would he want to do that? There was only one way to find out. 'Why do you want to attend?' she questioned suspiciously.

'I like weddings,' he replied without a blink. 'Provided they're someone else's.'

Lydie eyed him hostilely. Why would he want to gatecrash her brother's wedding? She thought of her beloved father, in his own private hell, and her eyes widened. 'You wouldn't embarrass my father?'

Jonah's smile abruptly disappeared. 'I have the greatest respect for your father,' he told her sternly.

She thought she could believe him. But, even so. 'I'd better sign something to the effect that it is I who owe you that money,' she suggested.

Jonah's harsh manner departed. 'I think I can trust you, Lydie,' he said evenly.

She had previously believed she could trust him—and had been set up for her pains. 'It isn't for you. It's for me,' she told him bluntly.

He looked back at her, his chin thrusting just that aggressive fraction forward. '*You* don't trust *me*?' he said coldly. 'You think, after the discussion we've just had, that I'll forget everything we've said, and that I'll send the debt collectors after your father?' Stubbornly she refused to back down. Silently a pair of obstinate clear green eyes stared into a pair of cold blue eyes. Then Jonah Marriott opened a drawer and drew out a sheet of paper. He dropped the paper down in front of her and without another word uncapped his pen and handed it to her.

He hates me, she thought, but was unshakeable in her resolve. That cheque had been made out to her father. She took the pen from Jonah and after a moment's thought wrote.

I, Lydie Pearson, in respect of the fifty-five thousand pounds borrowed from Jonah Marriott and paid into the bank account of Wilmot Pearson, hereby agree that the repayment of that fifty-five thousand pounds is my debt alone.

She read through what she had written and, while she felt lawyers might phrase it a little differently, she believed it said what she wanted it to say: that the debt was nothing to do with her father. Before she signed it, and purely as a courtesy, she turned the paper round so Jonah should read what she had penned.

It did not take him long. Though, when she would have taken the paper back and signed it, he took the pen from her hand and in his strong writing added something. Then, as she had, he turned it round for inspection. 'The fifty-five thousand pounds to be repaid at the direction and discretion of Jonah Marriott,' she read.

Lydie was not very sure of the ground she was on here, but, having stubbornly held out to have something in writing, she did not think she could start nit-picking about any wording now.

Without looking at him, she took the pen from him and signed her name at the bottom, and then added the date. She handed both pen and paper back to him, and watched while he recapped his pen and stood up. He was a busy man; her appointment with him was over.

'I take it you'd like a copy?' he queried.

Since the idea of that piece of paper absolving her father of the debt was her idea, she didn't know how Jonah could ask. In fact, she thought the original should be hers.

She stood up, chin tilted. 'Please,' she answered shortly.

He smiled that smile she was beginning to hate. 'I shall look forward to Saturday,' he said.

With that she had to be content. She would see him on Saturday—now how was she going to wangle him an invitation? And what possible excuse could she use for wanting him there? And what, in creation, was she going to tell her father?

CHAPTER THREE

LYDIE thought and thought all the way home. But she still had not worked out what to tell her father when she was heading up the drive of Beamhurst Court. She wanted to stick as close to the truth as possible, but doubted that her father would be impressed that his near to penniless daughter had claimed his debt as hers. He just would not stand for that.

The first person Lydie met on going indoors was her mother. Oh, grief. Her mother had not seemed very friendly towards Jonah Marriott when she had spoken of him. Lydie just knew she was going to ask quite a few vitriolic questions when Lydie said she wanted him to be invited to Oliver's wedding.

But there was a smile on her mother's face. 'Oliver's home,' she beamed, Oliver was home; all was right with the world. 'Did you leave your shopping in your car?' Shopping? 'Your father said you were going in to London to…'

'Oh, I couldn't see anything I liked.' Heavens, was there no end to the lies she had to tell?

'Nothing?' Her mother looked askance. 'In the whole of London?'

'You know how it is,' Lydie began uncomfortably, but was saved further perjury when Wilmot Pearson emerged from his study. Saved, that was, of lying further—to her mother.

'I'll go and see Mrs Ross about this evening's meal,' Hilary Pearson declared, and Lydie knew that whatever they had been going to have was about to be changed to something Oliver was particularly partial to.

In normal times she and her father might have exchanged wry smiles. But these were not normal times, and there was not a smile about either of them as her mother went to see their housekeeper and her father held his study door open—indicating that Lydie join him in there.

He was not interested in how she had fared on her shopping expedition, but as soon as they were in his study and he had closed the door he at once asked, 'When do we see Jonah?'

'We don't,' Lydie answered, but added hurriedly as her father's brow creased, 'I was lucky. I managed to see Jonah today.'

'You've s—'

'He was able to spare me a few minutes out of his busy day.'

'You told him that I wanted to see him?'

'Of course.' She was glad she hadn't had to lie about that.

'So you've made an appointment for me to…'

'Well, not exactly.' Her father was starting to look exasperated with her, and Lydie hurried on. 'He said you mustn't worry.'

'Not worry!' Wilmot Pearson stared incredulously at her, and Lydie rushed in again.

'He said to forget about the money.' What was one more lie?

'Forget it?' her father echoed, and, his pride to the fore, 'That I will not!' he stated vehemently.

'Oh, Dad, please don't…' she said helplessly.

And at her totally wretched tone he calmed down to stare at her. 'What…?' he began. She wriggled, mentally writhed, and knew she should have stayed away from the house until she had some convincing lie worked out. Though, the way things were, she felt it would be some time next week before she could come up with anything halfway convincing to relieve her father of his worry. 'Spit it out, Lydie love,' he coaxed, when she was still stumped.

'It's—difficult,' she said after a struggle.

'What is? I owe Jonah Marriott money and have to see him to discuss it. What's difficult about that?'

'That's just it! I don't want you to see him.'

Wilmot Pearson was a fair and just man. And, in respect of his two offspring, indulgent, and prepared to do everything he could for their health and happiness. Which was perhaps why he tempered what was obvious to him—that, regardless of what his daughter wanted, he and his pride demanded he meet with the man to whom he was in debt—and asked, 'Why don't you want me to see him, Lydie?' Oh, help. She racked her brain, but no good reason would come through. 'Why is it difficult?' he persisted.

'It's—difficult for me.'

'What's difficult for you?' he asked with what she thought was a father's admirable patience.

'Don't—er—don't make things difficult for me, Dad,' she said at last.

'For *you*?' he took up. 'Difficult for you? How?' he questioned. She could feel herself going pink, but it was more from feeling awkward and inadequate that she had no answer for him than anything else. But her father spotted her high colour and, having already noted that she seemed embarrassed to be having this conversation, 'Good Lord!' he exclaimed. 'You're blushing!' And, plainly looking for reasons for her blush, 'Surely—you haven't—fallen for him?' he pondered.

And suddenly, her brain racing, Lydie was ready to grasp at any straw her father gave her. 'Is—is that so astonishing?' she asked, hoping, when she couldn't meet her father's eyes, that he would think her shy of discussing this topic with him.

He thought about it. 'Well, I suppose not,' he to her surprise decided. 'You had a giant-sized crush on him when you were a teenager...'

'You knew about that?' she asked, astounded, at last able to meet his eyes. But, looking quickly away, she assured him, 'It isn't a crush this time, Dad.'

'Oh, baby,' he said, his own problems for the moment forgotten. 'But you hardly know him! Apart from seven years ago, you've only seen him twice recently.'

'Three times, actually. I saw him at the theatre on Saturday.'

'You went to the theatre with him?' he questioned. 'On *Saturday*, when you knew I wanted to see—'

'It wasn't like that,' she interrupted hurriedly. She didn't want her parent pursuing that track, but hoped he would think her reserve of old had reared its head, causing her to be unable to tell him anything about it either yesterday when she'd come home or at breakfast that morning. 'But anyhow,' she plunged on, grabbing at the fact that her father had taken one look at her mother and that had been that for him, 'how many times did you have to see Mother before you knew it was the real thing?'

With relief, Lydie saw her father had taken everything she said as gospel. They were away from the subject of that money anyway, and she guessed from his expression that he was recalling that his dear Hilary had not returned the compliment and fallen in love with him at first sight. She had taken some wooing, from what Great-aunt Alice had told her.

'And how does Jonah feel about you?' her father asked with a father's natural concern.

'I—it's too early to say,' she answered, winging it, playing it by ear—desperately glad Jonah Marriott wasn't a fly on the wall, listening to all of this. 'B-but he wanted to take me to dinner this coming Saturday.'

'He asked you for another date?' Lydie could feel herself colouring up that she had allowed her father to believe she had dated Jonah last Saturday. 'You didn't come home on Saturday night!' her parent remembered, looking a little shaken. And, while colour scorched her cheeks at that implication, she was thankful for once that hostilities were still prevailing between her parents, otherwise her mother would have told her father that their youngest was having a sleepover at her friend Charlie's.

'I had to tell Jonah that I couldn't have dinner with him because I'm unsure what time Oliver's wedding celebrations will go on until,' Lydie said in an embarrassed rush. 'Er—Jonah asked if he could—er—come to the wedding too.'

Her father looked at her solemnly for a second or two, and then he smiled. 'Well, that sounds as if he's keen enough,' he declared encouragingly. Lydie smiled faintly, very much confused that, purely in her father's interests, she had been able to make up this fantasy. 'You'd better ask your brother to see he gets an invitation.'

Lydie stared at her father. Agreed, she had been in very much of a lather, but it had been that easy? She was staggered. Well, that part of it had gone better than she had anticipated, but, 'And you won't say anything to Jonah? At the wedding, I mean. About the money?'

'It would hardly be appropriate,' he admitted. 'But you must see, Lydie, that I shall have to discuss it with him some time.'

She supposed she had known that. Her father was an honourable man. 'But not now, not until some other time. I think he's away this week,' she lied on the spur of the moment. 'Some conference or other. Abroad somewhere.'

'It will have to wait until next week, then,' her father agreed. But, looking at him, Lydie thought that although he was obviously still very much burdened, he suddenly did not seem to appear so hunched over as he had.

It was good to have Oliver home. He was a bit muddle-headed sometimes, but loveable—either because of or despite that. 'Lydie!' he exclaimed when she and her father left the study and went into the drawing room. 'How's life?' he asked, coming over and giving her a hug.

'Can't complain.' She grinned. 'Looking forward to Saturday?'

'To tell you the truth, I'll be glad when it's all over and Madeline and I can go off and be by ourselves. Such a fuss! I tell you, if it were left to me we'd just nip into a registry office somewhere and do the deed—but Mrs Ward-Watson will have none of it.'

'Of course she won't,' his mother chipped in. 'These things have to be done properly, Oliver. The Ward-Watsons can't have their only daughter sneaking off somewhere as if they've got something to hide.'

Oliver, it appeared, had endured more than one lecture on the subject and did not fancy another, even if it was from his adoring mother. 'Any sign of you trotting up the aisle yet, Lydie?' he asked, more to take the limelight away from himself than anything.

About to say no, that she was more interested in children than grown men, Lydie just then caught her father's glance on her. 'I…' she said, and faltered.

'You've gone red!' Oliver teased.

'Leave her be,' her father cut in. But, instead of making things better for her, succeeded in making her want to fall through the floorboards when he added, 'Though there is someone you could invite to your wedding.' Oliver looked at him, interested; her mother looked at him questioningly. 'Lydie's just started seeing Jonah Marriott. It would be a kindness if Mr and Mrs Ward-Watson sent him a wedding invitation.'

Oh, mercy! Lydie glanced to her mother, who was looking at her in total disbelief. 'How long's this been going on?' she asked sceptically.

'Lydie went to the theatre with him on Saturday,' Wilmot Pearson answered for her.

'I thought you went with Charlie somebody-or-other?' Hilary Pearson challenged her daughter.

'I—er—didn't think you—um—cared for Jonah,' Lydie answered, making out she had been lying then about her theatre date with Charlie, but pink with embarrassment that she was lying now.

'What have you got against Jonah Marriott, Mother?' Oliver chipped in.

'I'm going for a walk,' Lydie said—cowardly, but it saved her telling a whole load more lies— even if she did seem to be getting rather good at it.

Oliver, who was not seeing his fiancée that evening, seemed to spend most of his time on the telephone to her, but he made it to the table at dinnertime and seemed quite blissful.

Lydie was glad he was there. Her mother could not help that he was her favourite and Lydie was perfectly happy that it was so. Particularly that evening when, her mother finding yet more matters to quiz him over, it rather took any inquisitive questions away from Lydie herself.

'Jonah should get his invitation in the post tomorrow, by the way,' Oliver informed her at one point. 'You were still out walking when Madeline rang, but Dad was able to give me his address.'

'Oh, thanks,' she mumbled, glad her father had been able to find Jonah's address. She hadn't a clue where he lived.

Oliver and her parents were going to stay overnight in a hotel near his bride's home on Friday. This so they should not have far to travel the next day. The wedding was not taking place until the afternoon, so Lydie would have plenty of time in which to go and collect her great-aunt Alice. But there were days to be got through before Friday.

Uncomfortable with lies, but seemed called upon to tell them at every turn, Lydie wanted to keep as much out of her parents' way as possible. Which was why, on Tuesday, she did take herself off shopping for a wedding outfit.

She had some very nice outfits in her wardrobe, several of which would have been suitable, and she fretted for an absolute age about spending money she should give to Jonah Marriott. Then she decided that what she would spend would be a drop in the ocean compared with what she owed him. And somehow—and she was sure it had more to do with keeping out of her parents' way than the fact that Jonah would be a guest at the wedding—it seemed a good idea to shop for something new.

She returned to the home she so loved with several large glossy carriers. 'You really have been to town,' her mother quipped when she went in, and was as delighted as Lydie had been at the lovely deep coral suit and its accessories she had purchased.

Oliver was unable to keep away from Madeline the next day, and left early and came home late.

But he declared on Thursday that Mrs Ward-Watson had said they could cope very nicely without his assistance from then on—and Madeline, it seemed, had a hundred and ten things she must attend to before the 'big day'.

'Which leaves me having to ask my little sister to come and have a drink with me down at the Black Bull.'

'Since you ask so charmingly,' she accepted. Oliver's present friends were scattered around the country, apparently, but since some of them were converging on the same hotel tomorrow he was having his stag 'do' then—with strict instructions not to get up to anything too outrageous.

'Have you and Madeline decided where to live yet?' Lydie asked when sitting in the Bull with a gin and tonic. Oliver took a swig of his pint.

'Didn't Mother tell you?' He laughed sunnily at the thought that that must be a first. 'Madeline and I are having a place built in the grounds of her parents' home.'

'Will you like that?' Lydie queried slowly, her feelings more and more for her brother, whose life seemed to be being taken over by the Ward-Watsons.

'You bet your life I will,' he declared stoutly. And, misinterpreting her entirely, 'I'd much rather have something new and up to date.'

That shook her more than somewhat. 'You wouldn't rather have something with a bit of history to it?'

'Like Beamhurst?' He shook his head. 'No, thanks! All Dad's ever done is chuck money at the place. It's no wonder he's skint! That place costs a mint to keep in good repair.' And while Lydie stared at him, incredulous that he didn't seem to appreciate that their father was 'skint', as he called it, for no other reason than that he'd had to wade in there and rescue his son from his debts, Oliver went blithely on. 'I told him on Tuesday, when Mother was bleating on about my inheritance, that if my inheritance included the white elephant Beamhurst I'd be just as happy to be left out of the will. Drink up,' he said, 'I'll get you another.'

He left her sitting stunned, and went up to the bar while Lydie tried to accept that just because she loved the old house it did not necessarily mean that Oliver had to. Even if he had been brought up there. By the sound of it, too, Oliver was quite cheerfully unaware that, through the mismanagement of his business, their father was in an extremely severe financial situation. As she had been sublimely unaware of the parlous state of their father's finances, so—incredibly—had her brother been! True, with Oliver getting engaged

and wanting to be out of the house and off somewhere with Madeline all the while, it was doubt-
ful that he had been in the house for more than
half an hour at a stretch. But…

With her brother so excited and happy, and so
looking forward to marrying his Madeline, now
did not seem to be a good time to acquaint him
with a few pertinent details.

It was a relief to wave goodbye to her parents
and brother on Friday morning—a relief to be in
the house with just her and Mrs Ross. No need
to start getting uptight lest she be called on to
evade some truth or other—or even tell a down-
right lie. And what lies she had told, albeit in the
interests of her still very worried-looking father.
Those lies had been told ultimately for her
mother's peace of mind too.

But Lydie was plagued by the thought that,
come Saturday, she was somehow going to have
to make it appear that she and Jonah had been
'intimate friends' and that they were well on the
way to being 'an item'. Oh, save us! Then, should
she be able to overcome *that* mighty obstacle—
without Marriott Esquire being or becoming
aware that he had been designated her 'beau'—
she had to learn what he had come up with in
respect of the fifty-five thousand pounds she owed
him. One way and another Lydie could not say

that she was looking forward to her brother's wedding all that much.

Saturday dawned bright and beautiful and Lydie decided to go and call for her great-aunt in plenty of time. She was about to leave the house, however, when Charlie Hillier rang. 'I thought you might like to come and have a meal with me,' he said straight away, sounding just a hint not his normal self.

'When were you thinking of?' Lydie asked. He was a friend; she sensed something was troubling him.

'Tonight would be good.'

'Charlie! It's my brother's wedding today! I can't.'

'Sorry, I forgot. Tomorrow, then? Come to dinner.'

Fleetingly she thought of how she was supposed to be dating Jonah Marriott. Could she pretend to her parents that her date tomorrow was with him? Oh, Lord, she was getting herself into all sorts of bother here! 'I'd love to, Charlie,' she said quickly. 'Er—is anything the matter?'

He was silent, and she could almost hear him blushing when, all in a rush, he blurted out, 'That new woman—the one I told you about—Rowena Fox—she's asked me out!'

Poor Charlie, Lydie mused as she drove to her great-aunt's house. He was in one almighty flap. Without a doubt he would not mind at all going out with the unable-to-wait-to-be-asked Rowena, but with astonishing lack of self-confidence just knew something would go wrong if he did—and that Rowena would never stop laughing at him. Charlie was in urgent need of some confidence-bolstering. That, Lydie knew, would be her role tomorrow. Meantime, there was her brother's wedding to attend.

'Will I pass muster with your mother?' Alice Gough asked, ready and waiting when she answered the door to her great-niece.

'You look terrific!' Lydie beamed, admiring her great-aunt's silk dress and straw hat.

They did not leave straight away, Alice decreeing, 'I've made some sandwiches. We might as well eat them now. The formalities and photographs at these dos take for ever—heaven alone knows when we'll eat again.'

They were at the church in good time, and were ushered into their pew immediately behind Lydie's parents. Lydie smiled encouragingly as her rather strained-looking brother, who was seated in front of her parents with his best man, looked over his shoulder to her. Her mother too had turned in her seat, and Lydie saw her mother give her great-aunt the once-over—and spotted great-aunt Alice doing likewise. Both appeared satisfied, and Lydie and her great-aunt took their seats and awaited the events.

Lydie didn't know how her brother's insides were that morning, but hers were very definitely on the fidget. Why did Jonah Marriott want to come to the wedding anyway? Him and his, 'I like weddings. Provided they're someone else's.' He wasn't remotely interested in this particular wedding. He just wanted to make her sweat, that was all.

She was not too clear why he would want to make her sweat. What was clear to her was that she had never felt so on edge. She hoped he wouldn't come, that he would fail to turn up— and then realised that, should he not come, she would be the one left looking a fool. The things she'd invented to get him an invitation!

Lydie's great-aunt Alice had the seat nearest the aisle so that, being shorter than Lydie, she should have a good view of the wedding procession when it arrived. But Lydie's thoughts were more on Jonah Marriott, and her growing certainty that he would not come. She started to quite hate him—making her look a fool like that. Heaven alone knew what fresh lies she would now have to tell to cover his non-appearance.

Suddenly, though, she became aware that a tall man had strolled up the aisle and was standing at the entrance to their pew. She looked over to him, and her insides somersaulted. She was not sure her heart did not give a little flip too. He had come.

Their eyes met. He looked superb. Tall, immaculately suited, those fantastic blue eyes—not to mention he was extremely good looking—and sophisticated with it. 'Lydie,' he greeted her.

She flicked her gaze from him for a moment, and found her voice. 'Jonah, I don't think you know my great-aunt, Miss Alice Gough. Aunty, Jonah Marriott, a fr-friend of mine.'

'Pleased to know you, Miss Gough.' Jonah pleasantly shook hands with her and then moved into the pew to go in front of Lydie and take a seat beside her. Whereupon he bent close to her ear, and asked, 'Where's the boyfriend?'

Oh, help! All at once it struck Lydie like a bolt from the blue that, somehow or other, for today's purposes, she was going to have to tell Jonah that *he* was her boyfriend! Oh, heavens. Yet she just couldn't have him mingling with her family and referring to someone else as her boyfriend.

'Er...' she began, but was so overwhelmingly conscious of him sitting so close to her, and of what she must say to him, that she could get no further.

'Er?' he prompted—and her newly discovered thumping tendency was on the march again.

She would have liked to move her head away from the close proximity with his, but she could not afford to have anyone else hear what she had to say. 'I—um—need to talk to you—rather urgently—on that subject,' she said in a low voice.

'Shall we go outside?' he asked blandly, obviously picking up that she did not wish to be overheard.

She gave him a speaking look—she really was going to thump him before this wedding was over. 'For the purposes of today, and until I can explain,' she said through gritted teeth, '*you* are my boyfriend.'

His head came closer, and to her amazement he brushed aside her night-dark hair and planted a kiss on her cheek. 'Forgive me, darling,' he murmured, 'I forgot to do that when we said Hello.'

Thump him? She'd like to throttle him! Her insides were having a fine old time within her. He was playing with her; she knew that he was. And, having designated him her boyfriend, there was not one darn thing she could do about it!

She moved her head out of range, and gave him an icy look. He smiled. Lydie gave her attention to the printed Order of Service they had each been handed. 'Do you know these hymns, Aunty?' She concentrated on her great-aunt instead.

'Backwards,' her great-aunt replied. 'Is it serious?'

'What?'

'You and your man?'

Oh, grief. Lydie found she had the utmost trouble in lying to her great-aunt. 'I'm working on it.' She played for safety, saw and heard Alice Gough smile and then actually giggle, then the strains of Richard Wagner hit the air, and everyone got to their feet.

The ceremony was lovely. The bride looked radiant, and Lydie felt a lump in her throat as she witnessed her only brother being married. She saw her mother trying to be surreptitious as she reached for her handkerchief, and Lydie felt choked again when she spotted her father take a comforting hold of her mother's hand. Her father might have been very out of sorts with her mother all this week, with verbal communication between them at a minimum, but that did not mean they did not still care deeply for each other.

As they had always been going to have to—provided Jonah turned up, that was—he and her father met up with each other as they mingled outside of the church. 'How are you, Wilmot?' Jonah at once greeted her father, extending his hand.

Her father shook hands with him. 'I'm in your debt, Jonah. I think we should meet.'

Jonah nodded, his eyes on the man who had been a stone heavier and a lot healthier-looking the last time he had seen him—three years ago. 'May I call you?' Jonah asked.

'If you would.' And, turning to his wife who had appeared at his elbow, 'You remember Jonah?'

'Isn't it a perfect day?' Lydie's mother commented, evidently still uncertain whether to like her daughter's escort or not.

Jonah smiled politely, and looked at Lydie, 'Quite perfect,' he replied to her mother.

There was no time then, or for some while, in which Lydie could explain to him why she had let her family believe that she and he were dating. But while Jonah was undoubtedly waiting, and she did not lose sight of the fact that she had some explaining to do, Lydie noticed that her great-aunt had started to wilt, and her great-aunt became her first priority.

The wedding reception was being held at the bride's home, Alcombe Hall. But when Lydie and her great-aunt started to walk the quite some distance to where Lydie had been able to park her car, Jonah took charge and offered, 'My car's right here, Miss Gough.' And, before Lydie could say a word, he had opened up the passenger door and was helping Alice Gough in. Then Jonah was turning to the slightly stunned Lydie, his expression bland, but something indefinable lurking in his eyes. 'See you shortly, dear,' he said, and Lydie knew then that if he made the smallest attempt to kiss her cheek in parting she was definitely going to thump him.

She took a step away. He got the message and he drove off, and Lydie mutinied like crazy. First of all Marriott had arrived at the church *after* her, yet had still somehow found a favoured parking spot, and secondly that was *her* great-aunt he had just gone off with, not his.

By the time she had reached her car, though, Lydie was starting to wonder what in thunder was the matter with her. She should be grateful to him that, whether or not he too had spotted her great-aunt's look of weariness, he had saved her the need to walk quite some way. Lydie recalled how Jonah had said he had the greatest respect for her father. That had been evident in the manner in which he had spoken to him—and she *was* grateful to him for that.

So, it appeared that there was nothing the matter with Jonah other than that he was enjoying himself hugely at her expense—she could still feel the imprint of his mouth against her cheek. And why wouldn't he enjoy himself at her expense? He might have asked to be invited to this wedding, but he hadn't asked to be nominated her boyfriend. Which then brought what was the matter with her down purely to nerves. Fact one, she found him extremely unsettling. Fact two, she owed him all that money. Fact three, she hadn't even got a job yet, and any time now he was going to tell her his idea for how she should begin to pay him back.

Lydie pinned a smile on her face on arriving at Alcombe Hall. She joined Jonah and her great-aunt, who appeared to be getting on famously, and who had waited for her before tagging on to the procession waiting to shake hands and congratulate the bride and groom.

After which Jonah found a chair for her aunt and, with waiters hovering, accepted refreshment for the three of them. With everyone in happy spirits time went by, with more photographs—a good number having been taken at the church— and guests chatting and renewing old acquaintances until it was time for the meal and the speeches. But at no time did it seem the right time for Lydie to have a private conversation with the man who was, whether he liked it or not, her man-friend in particular that day.

Jonah had been placed in between Lydie and her great-aunt at the meal table, and Lydie had to give him top marks that he saw to it that her great-aunt was not neglected. He was attentive to her too, pleasant and affable, but it was still just not the place in which for them to discuss what they had to discuss.

Nor was there any space later, when the meal was at an end and all the speeches over and the guests started to move about. Because by then Lydie was thinking in terms of getting her great-aunt Alice home. She knew the dear love had en-joyed the wedding, but sensed she had had enough. And was certain of it when modern mu-sic started issuing forth from one of the rooms and her great-aunt visibly winced.

'You look worried?'

Lydie looked up to see Jonah addressing her. 'I think I should take Aunt Alice home, but...' She didn't have to finish.

He nodded understandingly. 'I'll come to your car with you when you're ready.'

Lydie supposed the drive of Alcombe Hall was as good a place as any on which to have their discussion. But it took them some while in which to say their courtesy farewells.

By then all Lydie could think of was that her great-aunt seemed to sorely be in need of rest and quiet. 'Take my arm, Miss Gough,' Jonah suggested when at last they were out on the drive. 'This gravel path is very uneven in places.'

'I'll go and bring the car up, you stay there,' Lydie attempted, but Alice Gough would not hear of it. They went very slowly to Lydie's car, and Lydie could not help but notice how heavily Aunt Alice leaned on Jonah. 'You'll stay and enjoy the rest of the—er—festivities?' Lydie asked him, for something to say as they progressed to her car. 'You—um—said you liked weddings,' she reminded him.

She looked across at him. His answer was to grin—and something happened in her heart region. Lydie did not speak to him again until they had safely assisted her great-aunt into the front passenger seat and, on their way to the driver's door, had walked to the rear of the car. And there Lydie halted. Jonah halted with her.

'I'm—sorry about you having to pretend to be my boyfriend today.' Having got started, she apologised in a rush.

'What was all that about?' he asked solemnly, and she was glad he was taking her seriously.

'Even now I'm not sure quite how it came about,' she confessed. 'When I got home, after seeing you on Monday, I had to own up to my father that I'd seen you and that you'd said he wasn't to worry about the money. That you'd said he was to forget about it. I know, I know—I lied again,' she inserted hurriedly. 'But my father's a very worried man, and he's hurting badly over this.'

'Hurting?' Jonah repeated. 'I'm sorry to hear that.'

'Anyhow,' she rushed on, 'he was adamant he would *not* forget about it, and, I don't quite know how, but he was insisting on seeing you—he still is—and I was saying something about it being difficult, that... Well, you know and I know that the debt is mine—' She broke off to take a look inside the car and with relief saw that here great-aunt was not fidgeting to go home but had nodded off to sleep. 'Anyhow, I said something to the effect that I didn't want him to see you.'

'And he, naturally, wanted to know why?'

She nodded. 'He insisted on knowing why. I again said it was difficult.'

'You were floundering.'

'I'm new to this telling lies business.'

'You seem to be doing exceedingly well at it.'

She did not thank him for that comment, and said in a rush, 'I was getting very hot under the collar by this time. Dad—um—noticed my warm colour and was certain I was blushing because… Well, he seemed to think I…' she faltered '…that I had fallen for you.' She was feeling very hot under the collar again by this time. 'Well, to be honest, I rather led him to think that,' she felt she had to confess. She had no intention of telling this sophisticated man of her father's comments about the crush she'd used to have on him. 'Well, what with one thing and another,' she rushed on, 'and I wasn't thinking, just working on instinct, I kind of gave my father the impression that I was seeing you—backed up by the fact you wanted to come to Oliver's wedding. He—um—seemed to think that made you—um—a bit keen on me,' she ended, her voice tailing off lamely.

'You *do* appreciate that I'm not in the running to be anyone's ''steady''?' Jonah asked gravely.

'Don't flatter yourself!' she snapped pithily, up in arms in a second.

He smiled that insincere smile, and her right hand itched. 'Having established that fact,' he commented, 'there seems little more to say.'

'Just a minute!' She halted him when she thought he might be thinking of walking away. 'We were going to discuss what you'd been able to think of in terms of me paying you that money back.'

'You want me to tell you now, how—?'

'Please,' she interrupted; she had waited nearly a week to hear. 'My own idea is to get a couple of jobs and make regular payments...'

'What sort of work were you thinking of?'

'Anything I can find. Nannying during the day, night-time too if I can find something. But, generally, I'm prepared to do anything.'

He eyed her steadily. 'Anything?' he questioned. 'You said anything?'

Of course, anything. He had saved her parents from having to move out from Beamhurst Court. 'Anything,' she agreed. But added quickly, 'Anything legal, that is.'

His mouth picked up at the corners—involuntarily, she rather thought. But he sobered, and asked, 'How old are you?'

She was sure he knew how old she was, but answered, 'Twenty-three. Why?'

He shrugged. 'Just making sure that anything I propose is quite legal—amongst consenting adults.'

She stared at him. 'I'm not too sure I like the sound of this,' she told him cuttingly.

He seemed amused, and she added awaking shin-kicking tendencies to her head-thumping tendency list. He looked from her to bend and look into the car, where her great-aunt, Lydie saw as she followed suit, was starting to stir from her doze. 'You know where I live,' Jonah began as he straightened up.

'I don't, actually,' Lydie told him.

Jonah took out his wallet and extracted his card, and handed it to her. 'You'd better come and see me tomorrow—at my London apartment.'

'Tomorrow? Sunday? At your home?'

'Yes to all three,' he replied, and she knew he was playing with her again.

'But I thought we were going to get something settled today.'

'Don't you think it would be kinder if you took your great-aunt home?'

He was right, of course, but it annoyed Lydie that he was presuming to tell her how to look after her great-aunt, even if he *was* right. Lydie looked at his card and saw that he had an address in London and he also had a house—Yourk House, to be precise—in Hertfordshire.

But she wanted this settled and done now. 'I can come and see you tonight?' she offered.

'Hmm, that might interfere with my plans for this evening,' Jonah answered pleasantly.

'Tomorrow will be fine,' Lydie said quickly, a funny sensation hitting her stomach that he was obviously seeing some elegant blonde at any time now. 'What time?' she asked. 'I can be with you just after breakfast.'

'I like to have a lie in on Sundays,' Jonah replied nicely. She'd like to bet he did! 'Let's see,' he contemplated. 'Come early evening.'

She was having dinner with Charlie tomorrow. 'I have a date tomorrow,' she was pleased to let him know.

'Really, Lydie! Two-timing me so soon?' he mocked.

She supposed she had earned that—he hadn't asked to be designated her boyfriend that day. But she waited. Though, when he did not suggest another time, she realised that he clearly expected her to cancel her date. 'What time early evening?' she capitulated.

'Shall we say—seven?'

'Seven,' she agreed, and turned from him.

He was there at the driver's door before her to—sardonically, she thought—open her car door for her. He wished her now awake great-aunt a pleasant journey home, and took a step back.

He had not closed the door, however, when Alice Gough's voice floated clearly on the air. 'What a very nice man, Lydie. He'll make some girl a wonderful husband.'

Suddenly speechless, Lydie looked from her great-aunt to where Jonah was standing with a look of mock horror on his face. Looking straight up at him, Lydie was glad to find her voice. 'Thank heaven it won't be me!' she tossed at him, and, slamming the door shut, she put her foot down and got out of there.

CHAPTER FOUR

WITH her great-aunt cat-napping for most of the way to Penleigh Corbett Lydie had plenty of space in which to reflect on the day. Though it was not thoughts of her brother and his lovely bride which occupied the major part of Lydie's mind, but Jonah Marriott.

Why he had wanted to come to the wedding was as much a mystery to her as ever. But come he had and, she had to admit, he had done nothing to let her down. Though that didn't alter the fact that she still had that sword of fifty-five thousand pounds dangling over her head. Heaven alone knew what Jonah would come up with—and would he be prepared to wait while she earned enough to pay him back?

Lydie drove at a sedate pace and it was a little after seven when they reached her great-aunt's home. Lydie went indoors with her, and was concerned enough about her great-aunt's lack of colour to suggest she wouldn't mind keeping her company overnight.

'That *would* be nice!' Alice Gough exclaimed. 'I don't see nearly enough of you, Lydie.'

Feeling a touch guilty that, for all she wrote regularly to her great-aunt, she could have visited her more often than she had, Lydie made a mental note that, no matter in which part of the country she would end up working, she would make all efforts to visit her more frequently.

They discussed the day's events, with Alice Gough asking, 'When are you seeing Jonah again?'

'Tomorrow,' Lydie answered truthfully, and her aunt smiled serenely.

'I think you'll do very well together,' she commented.

Lydie opened her mouth to state that there was nothing serious between her and Jonah Marriott, but her great-aunt was looking ready to doze again, and Lydie thought it might be a better idea to talk in terms of going to bed.

Aunt Alice decided she had eaten enough that day to last her a week and required nothing more than a warm drink. She insisted on making it herself, but did allow Lydie to make up her own bed. Eventually Lydie said goodnight to her but, not ready for sleep, she stayed downstairs.

Lydie pottered about, tidying up the kitchen and idly thinking of how her parents had decided to stay an extra night at their hotel. Out of consideration for their housekeeper, who was expecting her to return, Lydie got out her mobile phone and rang Mrs Ross to say she would not be home until tomorrow.

Next Lydie sat down to think about her meeting with Jonah the next evening. She was seeing him at seven, but owned she was feeling more than a shade uneasy about that meeting. Nor was she too thrilled either that, when he full well knew she had a date tomorrow night, the arrogant devil, without thinking about it, expected her to cancel it!

Well, she jolly well wouldn't cancel it, she thought mutinously. Surely the business they were to discuss—her repaying that colossal sum of money he had given her—would not take all evening? To her way of thinking, their meeting should be all over and done with by seven-thirty.

Then Lydie remembered the effortless way Jonah had of sparking her to annoyance, and of generally upsetting her. If the same thing happened in their half-hour discussion tomorrow, would she feel at all like leaving his apartment and going on to Charlie's? Charlie wanted dinner and sympathy over his problem with the forward Rowena Fox. Lydie understood his excruciating shyness. She had suffered similarly—still did hit a wall of shyness occasionally—but in the main had outgrown the affliction. So, while she had every sympathy with Charlie, and the shyness he unluckily had never outgrown, she could not help but ponder if, after a half-hour business session with Jonah—whom she suspected was a tough business negotiator—she would feel up to the task of boosting up Charlie's basement-level confidence.

Another five minutes of tugging at it and she picked up her phone. 'I can't make tomorrow after all, Charlie,' she told him straight away.

'Ooh, Lydie!' he wailed. 'What am I going to tell Rowena on Monday?'

'Do you want to go out with her?'

'Well, yes, I suppose I do. But—'

'But nothing, Charlie. Has she, Rowena, been out with any of your colleagues?'

'Not that I know of. Several have asked her, but so far as I know she turned them down.'

'So what does that tell you?'

Charlie thought for some seconds. 'I don't know,' he said at last.

Lydie had to smile. Charlie was older than her, but she felt like some agony aunt. 'It tells you she likes you.'

'But I'm tongue-tied when she's around—awkward; especially with women.'

'Which is precisely why she wants to go out with you and none of the others.'

'Why?' He didn't get it.

'Well, I'm only guessing here, but I'd say she has probably had enough of over-confident—um—perhaps pushy types. Maybe she feels more comfortable with someone who isn't wise-cracking all the time.'

'Do you think so?' Charlie asked in wonder.

Lydie had no real idea, but now wasn't the time, in this exercise of building up his self-esteem, to admit it. 'You've known Rowena for three weeks now. Rowena has known you for those same three weeks. Do you think she would have asked you out, in preference to any of the others, if she was not a little taken by your non-pushy manner?'

He thought about it for a little while. 'Shall I go, then, do you think?' he asked.

Dear Charlie. He had already agreed that he wanted to go out with Rowena. 'I think you should,' she assured him.

There was a pause while Charlie thought about it. 'Do you—do you think I shall have to kiss her?'

Oh, Charlie! 'You're twenty-eight, Charlie Hillier,' Lydie told him severely. 'And I am not your mother.'

He laughed, and they said goodbye the best of friends. To Lydie's way of thinking, with Rowena in charge of this date, she would let him know if she was expecting to be kissed. All he had to do was just be his loveable shy self.

Lydie was pleased to see on Sunday morning that after a good night's rest her great-aunt was looking so much better. With nothing pressing to get home for, Lydie stayed with her until after lunch, and then made her way back to Beamhurst Court.

With the time coming ever nearer when she must get ready to go to Jonah Marriott's apartment, a familiar churned-up feeling started to make its presence known. Lydie went upstairs to shower and to think what to wear. She had spent a little time last night in trying to build up Charlie's confidence—she wished someone would come and build up hers.

She was under the shower, so did not know that her parents had returned home until, dressed in a pale green trouser suit, her raven hair loose about her shoulders, Lydie went downstairs and heard sound coming from the drawing room.

With her shoulder bag in one arm, car keys in hand, she opened the door to find her parents relaxing there. 'Just off out?' her father asked with a smile for her.

'I'm going to see Jonah,' she answered.

'I wonder you bothered to come home,' her mother chipped in slightly acidly, and, as Lydie looked questioningly, 'Mrs Ross said you didn't come home last night.'

'I didn't think Aunt Alice looked too well,' Lydie explained.

'She looked all right from what I could see!'

'She seems to tire very easily,' Lydie explained.

'What do you expect?' Hilary Pearson demanded. 'She's eighty-one!'

Eighty-four, Mother! 'You didn't think she looked a little pale?'

'We're all a little pale. And likely to remain so,' her mother went on sniffily, with a baleful look to her husband, 'until this whole sorry mess is resolved.'

Lydie glanced over to her father, who was looking pained and tight-lipped. She felt that her mother could be kinder to him, but knew she could not interfere. Now seemed as good a time as any to be on her way. 'I'll see you later,' she said, adopting a cheerful tone.

'Would that be tonight or tomorrow morning?' her mother asked sourly.

And, while Lydie thought her mother meant that by the time she got in that night her parents would be in bed, her father was saying, *'Hilary!'*

in his newly found cross manner, causing Lydie to realise her mother was assuming that her daughter might spend the whole night with Jonah Marriott. Without another word Lydie left them and went out to her car.

She was driving out through the gates of Beamhurst Court before it all at once struck her what had brought on her mother's rancid comment. Her mother had not associated her nonreturn home last night with Aunt Alice, but had associated it with Lydie first dropping off Aunt Alice and then going to stay overnight at Jonah's apartment! Mrs Ross must obviously have commented to her that, with all of them being away, she'd had the house to herself last night. Her mother had, Lydie could see now, put two and two together—and had got her sums wrong. Lydie thought she had as good as told her mother that she hadn't come home last night because, concerned for Aunt Alice, she had stayed the night with her. Jonah, Lydie realised, had probably not gone back inside Alcombe Hall after seeing her and her great-aunt to her car.

Lydie groaned, the words 'tangled web' and 'deceive' floating about in her head. She began to wonder what she had started. Though, in fairness to herself, knew that she would never have gone to see Jonah in the first place if her mother hadn't misled her the way she so dreadfully had. But as her thoughts drifted on to her father, and how he was hurting inside, Lydie knew that, whatever it cost, she could not regret any of what she had done.

Her insides were in turmoil when she arrived at the smart building where Jonah had his apartment. She approached the security desk—and was expected. In no time, tummy butterflies turning into vampire bats, Lydie found herself at his door.

Almost as soon as she had rung the bell, Jonah opened the door. 'Come in, Lydie,' he greeted her, his glance flicking over her long-legged shape in her trouser suit, her long dark hair and green eyes. 'I should have known you wouldn't be bridesmaid.'

His comment took her totally out of her stride. 'W-why?' she asked, to her own ears sounding as witless as she suddenly felt. He was casually dressed—and dynamite with it!

'You're much too beautiful,' he replied as they ambled into his drawing room. 'No bride would want such competition.'

'It strikes me you know too much about women,' Lydie replied, some of her wits returning. Did he really think her beautiful?

'Alas, true,' he sighed. 'Can I get you a drink?'

'No, thank you,' Lydie replied primly. She wanted to keep a clear sharp head here. There would be figures to discuss and, she owned, she was not much of a business woman.

'You'll take a seat, I hope?' he invited urbanely.

Lydie glanced around the gracious room with its sofas, its luxurious carpeting, its pictures. She walked over to a high-backed chair and sat down. 'This probably won't take long,' she began. It was as far as she got.

'You're anxious to keep your date?' Jonah asked, not sounding too pleased about it—as though he would be the one to decide how long it would take.

'Actually, no,' she replied coolly—outwardly cool, at any rate. Already she could feel herself starting to boil. 'I cancelled—in your honour,' she added sarcastically.

Water off a duck's... 'You enjoyed the wedding?'

Lydie stared at him, almost asked what that had to do with why she was there—but abruptly realised that Marriott was in charge here, and there wasn't a thing she could do about it.

'Very much,' she replied with what control she could find. 'You?' she asked sweetly. 'You have a penchant for other people's weddings, I believe.'

She thought the corners of his mouth tweaked a little—as though she had amused him. But he did not smile and she knew herself mistaken. 'Have you been in touch with your aunt this morning?' he asked solemnly.

'Aunt Alice was a little tired yesterday, but she looked more her old self this morning,' Lydie informed him.

'You've seen her?' The man missed nothing. 'You went over to see her? She told me she lives in Oxfordshire.'

'It's not so far away. Though I didn't have to travel; I stayed overnight with her.'

Jonah stared at her, but she had no idea what she expected him to say, and experienced familiar thumping tendencies when he remarked, 'You've gone a fetching shade of pink, Lydie.' And accused, 'Now, what guilty secret are you hiding?'

'I'm not guilty about anything!' she denied—thank you, Mother! But when he just sat there waiting, she somehow—and she blamed him for it—found she was blurting out, 'My m-mother got hold of the wrong end, and instead of her two and two adding up to her believing I stayed the night at Aunt Alice's, as I intended, she seems to think I—er—spent it with you some...' Her voice tailed off. But, feeling extremely warm suddenly, she knew her hopes that having had his explanation he would leave it there were doomed to failure.

'And why would your mother think that?' he determined to know.

'I hate men with enquiring minds!' she erupted.

'Which probably means you're in the cart here, little Lydie,' he commented pleasantly. But insisted, 'Why?'

Lydie gave him a huffy look. 'I'm not here to discuss that!' she told him—a touch arrogantly, she had to admit.

Little good did it do her! He just waited. And she saw that if she wanted to get down to talking facts and figures, which she did, then the sooner she told him, the sooner they would get down to the nitty-gritty of how much per month he would expect from her salary.

She sighed heavily, but realised there was nothing for it but to make a full confession. 'If you *must* know,' she started, gone from merely feeling warm to roasting, 'I stayed over with Charlie the previous Saturday...'

'Charlie?' he interrupted. 'Charlotte?'

Lydie gave him a peeved look. 'Charlie—Charles.'

'You're saying you—slept over—at his place?' Jonah asked, his expression grim suddenly. 'He was the man you were at the theatre with?'

Lydie nodded. 'I do sometimes stay when—'

'Spare me the gory details!' Jonah cut in harshly. And reminded her, 'You were telling me why your mother should think *I*—entertained—you here last night.'

Entertained! That was a new name for it. He was not smiling. 'Well...' she began, and did not want to go on, but knew, blast him, that she had to. 'Well, you know most of it,' she suddenly exploded. 'It was after...when I got home last Monday, after seeing you in your office. Dad seemed to get the impression that you and I were an item...'

'An impression which you gave him.'

'Oh, shut up!' Lydie snapped, irritated. 'Anyhow, Dad seemed to think I'd fallen for you...'

'Because, for some obscure reason, that is what you let him believe.'

'If you don't stop interrupting I shall never get this out!'

'I won't say another word.'

Lydie borrowed one of her mother's sour looks and bestowed it on him. He did not so much as flinch—she'd have to get more practice. 'Anyhow, my father said something about me hardly knowing you, and how I'd only seen you twice recently, and I said it was three times, that I'd seen you at the theatre on Saturday. People are always misinterpreting me!' Lydie shrugged, feeling totally fed up by then. 'Anyway, Dad suddenly remembered how I hadn't come home on Saturday night—and there you have it.'

'He believes you spent the night with me?' Jonah asked, amazed.

Never had she felt more uncomfortable. 'Yes,' she mumbled, but went quickly on, 'After that, getting you a wedding invite was small beer.' She did not like the fact that, having come to an end, all Jonah did was stare at her long and hard. 'So there it is!' she fumed. 'And perhaps now we can get down to the details of how I'm going to repay my debt to you.' Her voice softened. 'I don't mean to sound ungrateful, Jonah. I am grateful to you; I really am. It's just that everything's been a bit nightmarish recently, and I've been called upon to tell lies which less than two weeks ago I wouldn't have dreamed of uttering.'

Jonah's harsh look all at once seemed to soften. 'Poor Lydie,' he murmured, and, relenting, he smiled a smile that rocked her, then said, 'Let's make a pact to always be truthful with each other.'

'I'd like that—I think. Even if it's—er—embarrassing?'

'Even if,' he stated.

'Fine,' she said, 'I agree.'

'So, for a start, you'd better dump Charlie.'

'Dump Charlie?' she exclaimed incredulously. 'Charlie's my friend!' she protested.

'Dump him!' Jonah instructed, his manner totally unyielding.

'Why?'

Jonah did not look as if he would answer, but after some cold seconds replied, 'All this is about money paid into your father's bank account—with no conditions on my part. You have created conditions in order to save your father more embarrassment. And I understand that. But, since you have claimed me to your family as your boyfriend and—not to be too impolite—your overnight lover—' as if he cared about being impolite, she fumed '—what you must understand is that I can't have you running around town staying overnight with some other man.' And, having succinctly explained that, he ended heavily, 'So, dump him.'

She could have told him that Charlie was not her friend in the boyfriend sense—but, hang it all, a girl had to have some pride. 'Do I go around telling you to dump your women-friends?' she protested instead.

'You're in no position to tell me to do anything,' Jonah replied bluntly, and, as the truth of that hit home, the fire went out of her. That was until, his tone more giving, he added, 'But, since I must be fair over this, I have to tell you I don't have any women-friends.'

'Much!' Lydie erupted. 'That was a mirage I saw you with at the theatre the other Saturday, was it?'

'I don't usually go around explaining myself, but with our total honesty clause established I don't mind telling you that my theatre date with Freya was one made before you claimed me.'

Lydie gave him a hostile look, but, as she recalled the stunning blonde, she found her curiosity needed to be satisfied. 'You won't be seeing her again?' she asked, then realised that sounded much too personal and as if she was interested, and added hurriedly, 'Not that it's any of my business.'

'True,' Jonah agreed, 'it isn't.' But went on to confide, 'I'm a bit jaded with the hunt, if you'd like more truth.'

Her eyes widened. 'You've given up women?'

His lip twitched. 'That wasn't what I said,' he corrected her. Then proceeded to send her rigid with shock, by continuing, 'From what you've said, it doesn't sound as if your parents will be too upset should you spend next weekend with me.'

First Lydie went scarlet, and then pale. Then realised that he could not possibly be suggesting what she thought he was suggesting. 'Er...' she mumbled, but found she was stumped to say more.

Jonah smiled—that insincere smile that she hated. 'I'm going to Yourk House, my home in Hertfordshire, next Friday evening. You can come with me,' he decided.

Lydie stared at him, a drumming in her ears. 'W-what for?' she found the breath to ask.

That insincere smile became a twisted grin. 'Use your imagination, Lydie,' he suggested charmingly.

This wasn't happening to her! It couldn't be happening to her! This sort of thing didn't happen to her! She strove valiantly to *block* her imagination. 'I'm not much of a cook,' she managed.

'You won't be spending much time in the kitchen,' Jonah assured her pleasantly. And when, dying a thousand deaths, she just stared at him, 'Oh, by the way,' he said, getting up and going over to an antique desk where he collected up a piece of paper, 'your copy of the agreement we made,' he informed her nicely, and, coming back, handed it to her.

Lydie took it from him and with a thundering heart read the part written in his hand—''The fifty-five thousand pounds to be repaid at the direction and discretion of Jonah Marriott'. She swallowed hard, and could remain seated no longer. 'This is how I'm to repay you?' she charged, looking him straight in the eye. 'By being your pl...?' She faltered. 'By becoming your plaything?'

'Plaything?' His innocent expression did not fool her for one minute. 'For fifty-five thousand you'd be a pretty expensive plaything, wouldn't you agree?'

'What, then?' she demanded.

'Let's say that, ponder on the problem though I have—and I have to confess I'm not too enamoured of the idea of you working night and day nannying to—um—clear accounts—I have been unable, as yet, to come up with anything.'

'You think my going away with you this weekend might give you some ideas?' As soon as the words were out she blushed.

'Oh, yes,' he answered, his mouth picking up at the corners, his eyes on her crimson face. 'You could say that.'

He was teasing her, tormenting her—and he held all the high cards, and she didn't like it. But she had had his money, and her father was one very worried man.

'Why?' she challenged. 'Why do I have to come with you?'

'Why not?' he answered. 'As of now you no longer have a boyfriend—presumably your ex-boyfriend knows none of your financial business…?'

'Of course not!' she butted in. 'As if I'd tell anyone of the fix my father was in!'

'So what else would you do with your weekend?'

'Begin looking for a job for a start!'

'Don't do that. Not just yet. Let's get all this settled first. You'll feel much better about everything once we've had chance to fully probe into the whys, wherefores and all the possibilities of all this.'

'You're trying to tell me that to investigate possible areas, ways of my repaying you, is what this coming weekend is all about? And don't forget we have a ''complete honesty'' clause,' she reminded him.

'Would I lie to you, Lydie?' he asked smoothly. And she knew that was as far as she was going to get, particularly when he said, 'I'll finish work early on Friday, and call for you around six.'

'That won't be necessary, I have the address!' she exclaimed quickly, and saw him hide a smirk that, from what she had just said, she had agreed to spend the weekend with him.

'I'll drive you…' he began, but she was shaking her head.

'Sorry to be blunt, Jonah,' she butted in, while wondering why on earth she was apologising, 'but I would much prefer that you kept far away from my home.'

She had thought he might be offended, but he was more understanding than offended when he quietly replied, 'I saw for myself how drawn your father is, how he's suffering in all of this, Lydie, but I shall have to see him, talk to him some time.'

She felt awkward. She did not like Jonah's suggestion for the weekend any more now than she had ten minutes ago, but the great respect Jonah had for her father was there for her to see, and— mentally anyway—she had to thank him for it.

'I know,' she agreed. 'But not just yet. Not until we've got something worked out.'

He accepted that, or appeared to. 'Until Friday,' he said. She moved to the door, their meeting over. He walked with her. She looked at him as he opened the door for her to go through. Wonderful blue eyes met hers full on, and her heart seemed to go into overdrive. Then he grinned, a grin full of devilment. 'Try not to fret, Lydie,' he bade her. 'Who knows? You might have a fun weekend.'

'Did I tell you the one about flying pigs?' she snapped, and went quickly from him.

Her thoughts were intensely agitated on her drive home. She remembered thinking on the outward drive about how her father was hurting inside, and how she knew that, whatever it cost, she could not regret any of what she had done. That thought haunted her all the way back to Beamhurst Court—she'd had no idea then just how much it was going to cost. She was spending the weekend with Jonah at his home in Hertfordshire—he was not expecting her to cook.

Lydie was still in mental torment when she awakened on Monday morning. She swung first one way and then the other. Perhaps Jonah did not have in mind what she thought he had in mind. Wishful thinking? He had never made a pass at her, had he? And apart from shaking hands and giving her that kiss on the cheek in church on Saturday—and she rather thought she had asked for that, telling him he was her boyfriend—he had never touched her. Certainly he had not

given her the smallest hint that he might be thinking in terms of her being his bed companion.

Oh, grief! Even thinking about it made her go
hot all over. By the sound of it Jonah had wearied
of the chase, but it had to be faced—he was still
one all very virile male. And, while she had no
evidence that he even fancied her—and surely she
would have picked up some clue somewhere
along the line—was she so naïve as to believe that
this weekend had nothing to do with—bed?

Oh, heavens, she was having kittens just thinking about it, and found that the only way she
could cope was by trying to believe that nothing
of a sexual nature was going to take place between them that weekend. Jonah had said that, in
the absence of him being able to come up with a
plan of how she should repay him, they could
spend time this weekend probing possible ways
in which she could start making repayments.

Well, she couldn't think of anything, and if he
wasn't enamoured of her nannying night and day
in order to repay him she had no idea what his
superior business brain might come up with—
even if this coming weekend should stretch on to
Christmas.

Lydie went down to breakfast and found her
parents already in the breakfast room. But there
was such a strained atmosphere that, coupled with

guilt and fear, plus apprehension in case one of her parents should ask a question which might call for an embroidered answer, she just grabbed up a banana and, uttering something about washing her car, left them.

Jonah was on her mind the whole of the time while she washed and wax-polished her car. She should start looking for another job. Jonah didn't want her to do that, not just yet, he had said, when to her mind the sooner she started earning, the sooner she would start to repay him.

She went indoors and decided to ring Donna, her friend and ex-employer. Donna had been nervous of coping without her, but, while Donna had her phone number, Lydie had felt it better to leave it a while before ringing her.

'How is everybody?' Lydie asked when Donna answered.

'We're fine. Though I almost rang you several times.''

'I knew you'd cope beautifully,' Lydie said confidently.

'Which is more than I did. But we seem to have settled into something of a routine. How did the wedding go?'

Guiltily Lydie realised that she'd had so much else on her mind she had almost forgotten about Oliver's wedding—was it only two days ago? 'It was super,' she told Donna. 'Madeline looked lovely.' Unbidden, the memory winged in of Jonah saying yesterday, 'I should have known you wouldn't be bridesmaid. You're much too beautiful'.

'...job yet?'

'Sorry?'

'I was asking if you've got any work lined up yet. Only Elvira Sykes is back—you remember her? Well, she's home from Bahrain, and is desperate to have you if you're interested. She's constantly asking me for your phone number, which I keep telling her I've mislaid.'

'I haven't any work plans at the moment,' Lydie hedged.

'I'll tell her you're taking a long vacation and that if she isn't fixed up by the time you get back you'll give her a ring.'

They chatted on comfortably until one of the children started yelling, then said goodbye. Lydie wandered over to her bedroom window and, glancing out, saw that her father was mowing one of the lawns. Her heart went out to him—they had always employed a gardener, but apparently her father had had to let him go.

She saw her mother come out of the house, then spotted her mother's car on the drive; she was obviously off to some coffee morning, good works, or shopping. She got into her car without attracting Wilmot Pearson's attention. Lydie saw none of the affection between them that had been there on Saturday, when her father had taken a hold of her mother's hand.

Lydie consoled her disquieted feelings by musing that they had probably discussed their plans for the morning over breakfast, and, anyway, had her mother called to him her father would never have heard with the engine of the sit-on mower going at full pelt.

Then the phone rang and Lydie came away from the window. On the basis that her mother was out, her father was out of hearing and Mrs Ross was probably busy, Lydie, though assuming the call would not be for her, went and answered it.

The call was not for her, but that did not stop her heart from picking up its beat when she heard Jonah Marriott's voice. 'Hello, Lydie,' he opened. 'Is your father there?'

'You want to speak to him?' she asked sharply.

There was a pause at her sharp tone. 'If you've no objection,' Jonah replied smoothly.

She wasn't having this. 'What do you want to speak to him about?' she demanded. 'And don't tell me it's none of my business, because—'

'Oh, my word, what a little protector you are,' he cut in mockingly, but sobered to instruct, 'Put your hackles down, Lydie. I promised your father I'd be in touch. I'm just ringing to let him know I shall be out of the country for most of this week.'

Lydie calmed down a trifle. 'I'll tell him,' she said.

'He's not around?'

'It would take me ages to get him—he's mowing the lawn near the end of the drive. It would take me some minutes to get there—and you're a busy man.'

'And you're so considerate of my time.'

He wasn't going to speak to her father, no matter how sarcastic Jonah Marriott became. 'I'll give him your message,' she answered.

'We'll talk next week, your father and me—when you and I come back from Yourk House.'

Her insides did a flip. 'I'll—tell him,' she promised.

'And I'll see you Friday.'

She swallowed hard. 'I'll look forward to it,' she lied.

'What happened to ''always truthful with each other''?'

There was no answer to that. 'Goodbye, Jonah,' she said, and quietly put down the phone to find that she was trembling. And that was from just speaking to him! Heaven alone knew what she would be like on Friday!

She felt in need to do something positive, so went and showered off from her car-cleaning endeavours, and changed into jeans and a tee shirt, and then went to see her father. He was still sitting on the mower, but stopped the machine when, almost up to him, he spotted her.

'Jonah phoned,' she informed him. 'He wanted to speak to you...' Her father was off the machine with the speed of a man thirty years younger and Lydie hurriedly halted him. 'He's gone now!' Her father's face fell. 'But he asked me to tell you that he'll be out of the country for this week, but that he'll talk with you next week.'

Her father looked defeated suddenly. 'This can't go on,' he said, and seemed so utterly worn down that she just could not take it.

And she, who found lying abhorrent, was rushing in to tell him, 'Actually, Dad, Jonah has some proposition to put to you which he said will be— er—the answer.'

Her father brightened a little. 'He has?' he questioned, a little life coming back into his defeated eyes. 'What is it?'

'He wouldn't say,' Lydie went on, and even while her head was screaming, Stop it, stop it, don't say any more, she heard her own voice saying cheerfully, 'But whatever it is Jonah is certain—subject to your agreement, of course—that his proposition will be the answer to all your worries.'

'He said that?'

How could she say otherwise? More life was coming into her father's face. 'You know Jonah,' she answered.

'I certainly do. I've thought and thought until I wondered if I was going mental, and I can't see a way out of the hole I'm in. But if anyone can think up a way, I'd lay odds Jonah, a man with more up-to-date business know-how than most, would be the man to do it.' Already, in the space of seconds, her father was starting to look more like the father she knew. He had hope. 'Jonah wouldn't tell you more than that?' her father pressed. And at the urgency of his tone the enormity of what she had just done began to attack her.

'Afraid not,' she replied, marvelling that when she had just done such a terrible thing she should sound so cheerful. Somehow, though, she could not regret giving her father that hope. But, knowing she had told enough lies to last her a lifetime, she began to fear he might dig and dig away at her, and cause her to tell him yet more lies. She decided to make herself scarce. 'I was thinking of driving over to see Aunt Alice,' she said, which was true. She *had* been thinking of going to see her—tomorrow. 'I thought I'd go now, before she settles down for her afternoon nap.'

It was a relief to be away from the house, where unthought lies seem to pour from her as if of their own volition. Though when she thought of how her worried father's dead eyes had come to life on hearing that Jonah had thought up something, Lydie still could not regret it.

At worst her father would be back where he started when next week he and Jonah had their talk and Jonah told him that he had no answers. But at best—and that was the part Lydie could not feel too dreadful about—her tormented father had hope. His spirits had lifted, she had seen it happen. And now, for a whole week, while his financial worries would still be there to plague him, her lies had in effect lifted that dark ceiling of depression that hung over him night and day.

Her own spirits lifted when she found her great-aunt tending her beloved garden and, while still a touch pale, looking in otherwise good health.

Guilt over the lies she had told was lurking, however, and over the next few hours more guilt arrived in great swathes to torment Lydie. Oh, what had she done? Given her father a little peace of mind, but for what? Somehow she was going to have to own up to him before he and Jonah had that talk next week.

It was guilt and a feeling of not wanting to take away her father's peace of mind—not just yet anyway—hadn't he suffered enough?—that kept her away from Beamhurst Court until Thursday. She and her great-aunt enjoyed each other's company and it was a small thing for Lydie—who had with her only the clothes she stood up in—to rinse through her underwear to dry overnight and borrow one of her great-aunt's blouses.

'You're sure you have to go,' Alice Gough asked, but immediately apologized. '"More wants more",' she quoted. 'I'm a selfish old sausage. Love to your mother,' she said sweetly, to make Lydie laugh, and laughed herself, and Lydie hugged her and kissed her and said she would come again soon.

Lydie drove home, her few lie-free days with her great-aunt over, and two very big questions presenting themselves. One, however was she going to tell her dear father about her lies? The other, how on earth could she get out of going to Jonah Marriott's Hertfordshire home tomorrow?

The answer to the one question, she realised the moment she saw her father, was that she just

could not confess. How could she? He was looking so much better than he had. How could she
shatter that ray of hope he was clinging on to?

The only answer, as she saw it, was to give her
father a few more days of feeling that little bit
better about everything. Unfortunately, she could
find no answer to her reluctance to go to Yourk
House to meet up with Jonah tomorrow. Unless
there was some devastating earthquake in
Hertfordshire, an area not known for devastating
earthquakes, she would have to go.

It rained on Friday. The weather matched
Lydie's spirits. Her heart might be beating twenty
to the dozen whenever she thought about staying
at Yourk House that night, that weekend, but she
packed a bag for the trip without enthusiasm.

Since she could not just disappear for the weekend without giving her parents some idea of
where she was going—and Lydie had to admit
that to lie and say she was staying the weekend
with Aunt Alice had crossed her mind—Lydie
owned up that she was meeting Jonah at his
Hertfordshire home.

Her mother's lips compressed, but she said
nothing, and Lydie's father looked as though he
might say something to the effect that perhaps
Jonah might bring her home. But, clearly believing that if she was meeting him at his home then

it must mean Jonah was flying in from abroad and that Lydie would be driving her own car to meet him, he said nothing. But Lydie did not miss that her father seemed buoyed up with hope.

It was, of course, unthinkable that anyone else should know of their problems, and her mother, being the chairperson of an antiques society, was chief organiser in setting up a meeting that evening. Lydie was grateful that her father was going along for support and that both her parents left the house around five. She would not have to see them again before she left—her conscience and the lies she had told were getting to her.

Jonah had suggested he would pick her up at six and she had turned down his offer, but she decided that six was as a good a time as any for her to set out. With weekend bag in hand, she went down the stairs. But, having wished their housekeeper goodbye, Lydie was about to leave the house when the phone rang.

With hope in her heart that it was Jonah, ringing to cancel the weekend, Lydie went back to answer it. It was not Jonah but Muriel Butler, her great-aunt's neighbour, ringing to say that Miss Gough had been taken ill and that the doctor was with her now.

'What's wrong?' Lydie asked quickly, all thought of Jonah and everything else gone from her head.

'It's her heart, I think. I saw her collapsed in her garden from my upstairs window. She's had one or two little turns recently. But this looks serious.'

Lydie didn't wait to hear any more. 'I'm on my way,' she said, and was.

With her thoughts concentrated solely on her great-aunt, Lydie had been tearing along for about fifteen minutes when it suddenly dawned on her that the sleek black car that had been behind her had been there for the last five of those minutes. It was a car that could have easily outrun hers, and as easily have overtaken her, yet the driver seemed content to stay tucked in behind her. Then it was that Lydie realised she knew that car. It was the same car that had taken Aunt Alice from the church and to Alcombe Hall last Saturday. It was Jonah's car!

With no idea of why he was there, only a gladness in her heart to see him, Lydie pulled into the first lay-by she came to. Jonah pulled in behind her.

Intending to stop only to give him the quickest explanation of why she would not be visiting him at Yourk House that evening, and then be on her way, Lydie got out of her car as Jonah left his.

'If you're that eager to see me,' he commented obviously referring to the speed she had been travelling at, 'you're going in the wrong direction.'

'I'm not on my way to see you,' she replied solemnly. 'I can't come after all. My—' It was as far as she got.

'You're not coming!' He seemed more than a touch put out. 'We agreed...' he began, then spotted her weekend bag reposing on the back seat where, hardly knowing she still had it with her, she must have tossed it when she had raced to her car. And to her consternation he was instantly furious, as he tore into her harshly, 'You never did intend to come to Yourk House this weekend, did you?' And, while she just stood there, blinking at his fury, 'All that guff about preferring I kept away from your home!' he snarled. 'You knew in advance, way back last Sunday, that you wouldn't be home when I called!'

'Don't be—'

'Well, let me tell you, Lydie Pearson.' He chopped her off again, his chin thrust aggressively forward. 'No one cheats on me—*ever*!'

'I'm not—'

'Where are you going?' he demanded, suspicion rife.

But she had had enough, and heartily wished she had never stopped to tell him anything. 'That's none of your business!' she hurled at him angrily, and without more ado stormed from him and got into her car.

Seconds later she was charging on her way. The pig! The perfect pig! Fuming, she kept her foot hard down on the accelerator. She glanced in her rearview mirror—he was right behind her. So much for her telling him it was none of his business! From the look of things, the man who did not like to be cheated was *making* it his business!

CHAPTER FIVE

LYDIE arrived at her great-aunt's house in record time—so too did Jonah Marriott. Her great-aunt did not have a drive or a garage; Lydie parked in the roadside; Jonah parked behind her.

She hurried to Alice Gough's garden gate, and found Jonah there to open it for her. She ignored him and went through, just as Muriel Butler came out of her house and looked over the low dividing hedge.

'The doctor called an ambulance. They've taken Miss Gough into hospital. Heart attack,' she added.

'Thank you for ringing me.' With fear clutching at her, Lydie managed to stay calm. 'Which hospital, do you know?'

Lydie waited no longer than to hear which hospital the ambulance had taken her great-aunt to and, thanking Muriel Butler again, turned and hurried back down the garden path.

All this time, though Lydie supposed it had only taken a minute, Jonah had remained silent. But he was there to open the gate again, and had clearly learned in that minute all there was to learn. He took charge.

'We'll go in my car,' he stated. Lydie was in no mind to argue.

They made it to the hospital in less time than it would have taken in her car. Whereupon Jonah again took charge, finding out where Miss Alice Gough was, and escorting Lydie to the intensive care unit where her great-aunt was still being assessed.

They waited outside—it seemed an awfully long wait—and strangely, despite having felt fairly murderous towards Jonah in that lay-by, Lydie discovered she was glad that he was there.

He was there by her side when the doctor came from the ward and gave the news that there was not much chance Miss Gough would survive the attack.

Naturally Lydie refused to believe it. 'May I see her?'

'Of course,' he answered kindly. 'She's unconscious, but please go in.'

Somehow Lydie found she was holding tightly on to Jonah's hand. He made no attempt to retrieve his hand but went with her into the ward, where Alice Gough lay looking so pale, and so still. Lydie saw for herself that the doctor had been speaking only the truth.

Lydie sucked in her cheeks not to cry, and let go Jonah's hand to hold her great-aunt's hand. They stayed with her some minutes, then Lydie tenderly kissed her and, with Jonah, went outside.

'I should let my mother know,' she said to Jonah; it hadn't seemed right to her to discuss the matter over her great-aunt's bed.

'I'll ring her,' Jonah offered.

Lydie shook her head. Most oddly, she didn't want Jonah to leave her just then. 'They're not in—my parents. They're at a meeting. My mother will have her mobile switched off.'

'Tell me where and I'll go and get them.'

Lydie looked at him then, and fell in love with him. 'Oh, Jonah!' she cried, and he put a comforting arm about her.

'Be brave, sweetheart,' he urged softly.

'It was only yesterday that Aunt Alice was making me laugh when, as I was leaving, she asked me to give her love to my mother. She laughed too.'

'Remember her that way,' he suggested.

She's not dead yet! Lydie wanted to tell him furiously, and realised then that her emotions were all over the place. 'I'll go and sit with her. Could I ask you to ring Mrs Ross, our house-keeper, and ask her to tell my parents what has happened?'

'Of course,' he replied, and, the use of mobile phones banned in the hospital, he left her to go in search of a landline telephone.

Her parents arrived just after eleven. Jonah greeted them and then left the ward so the three family members should keep their vigil. Lydie's great-aunt died at eleven-thirty, and Lydie said goodbye to her.

She left her, left the ward, and found Jonah waiting outside. He took one look at her and held out his arms. Numbly she went forward. She was still cradled in his arms when her parents left the ward. Her father took charge.

'I'll see to things here, Lydie.' He looked at Jonah; now was not the time to discuss his finances. 'Perhaps you'll see Lydie gets home safely, Jonah?'

'I will,' Jonah answered.

In something of a daze Lydie went with Jonah out to his car. She wanted to weep, but wanted to weep alone. Tears were near. The only way to stem them was to think of something else.

She recalled she was supposed to be going to spend the weekend with Jonah at Yourk House. 'I—er—would you mind if we cancelled this weekend?' she asked in a hurry, not thinking, just talking.

'Consider it done,' Jonah replied calmly. 'I'm sorry I was such an evil brute in that lay-by,' he apologised.

In her view, by being there, staying there with her all these hours, he had more than made up for his evil brutishness. 'You weren't to know I was on my way out to drive to your place when Aunt Alice's neighbour rang to say she had been taken ill.' And, just then noticing the road they were on, 'Could you drive me back to my great-aunt's house, please?'

'You don't want to go home?'

'I—it doesn't seem right, somehow. I can't explain it. It just feels as if I'd be abandoning Aunt Alice if I went home now. As if I'd forgotten her.'

Jonah altered the car's direction. 'You were always sensitive,' he murmured, and drove her to Penleigh Corbett.

Having been with Jonah through the last many sad hours, having witnessed his attention—not least the way he had held her gently in his arms just now, not saying anything, but just holding her safe—Lydie realised that *he* was far more sensitive than he would want anyone to know.

'Do you intend to stay the night here?' he asked when they reached her great-aunt's house.

'Yes,' she confirmed.

'Would you like company? I don't mean bed company,' he assured her.

'I know,' she answered, love for him welling up inside her. 'I think I need to be on my own.'

He understood, and she loved him for that too. 'You have a key?'

'Third flowerpot from the left.'

There was a light on in the next-door house, and Muriel Butler suddenly appeared with the house key, having locked up after the ambulance had left, her face falling when Lydie told her the sad news.

'I'll stay here overnight,' Lydie added.

'If you need anything, anything at all, I'm only next door,' Muriel offered, but, not wishing to intrude, said goodnight and went back indoors.

'You go in. I'll get your bag from your car,' Jonah instructed Lydie, seeming to remember she had been in such a rush to leave her car she had not waited to lock it. 'Shall I have your car key? I'll lock it up,' he suggested.

Lydie gave him her key and went into her great-aunt's house, where a very short while later Jonah joined her.

'Thank you, Jonah, for...' she faltered '...for being there,' she said.

He came closer, his fantastic blue eyes searching into hers. 'You'll be all right if I leave you?'

Lydie nodded, and swallowed hard on emotion when he placed his hands on her arms and gently placed a kiss on her brow.

She telephoned her home after he had gone. She knew Mrs Ross would be in bed, but her mother always checked the answer-machine when she got in. Lydie left a message letting her parents know where she was. Then Lydie broke down and cried.

She wept for her great-aunt's passing, and for the love she had for her. Much later she was able to find a weak and watery smile through her tears that her great-aunt's passing had shown a tenderness in Jonah which Lydie had never suspected he had.

By morning she had adjusted only slightly that she would never again share her great-aunt's company, nor hear her have a sly, if funny, dig at her mother. Lydie wandered around the small semi-detached house and still felt her aunt's presence there. It was a comforting presence.

It was still early when her parents telephoned. She spoke with both of them, her father telling her to come home when she was ready, and also letting her know that he and her mother would be making all the arrangements about her aunt's funeral. 'I know you were fond of her, but try not to be too upset,' he said, and passed the phone to her mother.

'Are you on your own?' Hilary Pearson enquired, her voice less tart than it had been of late.

The question threw Lydie for a moment, until she recalled all that had gone on—the lie she had let her parents believe that she was not a stranger to spending a night with Jonah.

'Yes,' she answered, feeling slightly amazed that her sharp-as-a-chef's-knife mother should be so easily taken in. Although, on thinking about it, Jonah had been there with her at the hospital, and both her parents had seen her in his arms last night when they had come from Aunt Alice's bedside.

'Well, I expect you'll be seeing Jonah today,' her mother went on confidently, and, repeating what her father had said, tacked on a kindly meant, 'Try not to be too upset,' adding, before she rang off, 'The old dear had a good innings.'

Lydie put the phone down and supposed she should start thinking in terms of going home. But she was not yet ready; she felt restless and unsettled. She tidied round her great-aunt's already immaculately tidy home—Lydie had vacuumed and polished on Wednesday while her great-aunt just 'did a bit in the garden'.

Lydie smiled at the memory, and found more chores to do. By half past nine she had both beds stripped and the washing machine busy. There was a ring at the doorbell. She went to answer it. It was Jonah!

For ageless moments she just stared at him. She had wondered several times that morning if, in the trauma of last night, she had imagined her feelings for him. But with her heart pounding, her insides all squishy just from looking into his sensational sensitive blue eyes, Lydie knew she had imagined nothing. She was in love with him. It was a love that was there to stay.

'I thought you'd be somewhere in Hertfordshire!' she exclaimed, inanely, she felt, as she tried to get herself together.

'I can go to Yourk House another time,' he replied easily. And, those superb eyes studying her, 'I wondered if I could help in any way?'

Oh, Jonah! Sensitive, had she said? He was warm and wonderful—and she had better buck her ideas up. 'My parents have phoned. They're taking care of all the arrangements.'

He nodded, looked at her, and then nicely enquired, 'Do you know anywhere around here where a man might get a cup of coffee?'

'Oh, Jonah, I'm so sorry!' Lydie exclaimed. He had driven from London—and she had kept him on the doorstep! 'Whatever was I thinking of?'

He smiled kindly, his eyes on her slightly red-rimmed eyes. 'You have other matters on your mind,' he excused.

'Please, come in,' she bade him, and led the way to her great-aunt's sitting room feeling guilty—Lydie was growing no stranger to guilt. While she guessed he had noticed she had shed tears, she had not had thoughts of her great-aunt on her mind when talking to him. 'I'll just go and make some coffee,' she remarked.

'I'll come with you.'

'I've got the washing machine on. I think it came out of the Ark. It makes a fearful racket.'

His lips twitched. 'I can hear it,' he replied, and went into the kitchen with her, where a minute later the washing machine went on to a quieter cycle. 'Going home today?' Jonah enquired casually.

'Later,' Lydie agreed. 'There are a few practical things I should do here first.'

'Such as?'

'Well, somebody's got to sort out Aunt Alice's belongings. I think she would want me to do it...' Lydie shrugged helplessly, feeling very much out of her depth. 'Only it doesn't seem right to me, you know, when it was only last night that she died, to straight away pack up her belongings.' She paused, then confided, 'I really don't want to do it today.'

'Does it have to be today?'

Lydie thought about it. 'Well, I suppose not. Knowing Aunt Alice I'm certain she'll have her rent paid until the end of the month, so I've several weeks before I need hand the keys over to the local authority.'

'Then today you can rest and adjust.'

'I can?'

'You don't have to be in work on Monday, or for several Mondays yet,' Jonah pointed out logically. 'Why not leave it until you've said a formal goodbye to your great-aunt?' Lydie stared at him. It made sense to wait until after Aunt Alice's funeral. By then perhaps she would have adjusted a little. 'It's a sad time for you,' Jonah commented softly, and suggested, 'Spend the day with me?'

Her heart suddenly began to thunder. 'Spend the day with you?' she repeated faintly.

'Prior to your great-aunt's heart attack you were going to anyway.'

'That's true,' Lydie agreed, and rushed in at the gallop, 'I d-don't know what p-plans you had for this weekend, but—but I don't want to spend any t-time in bed with you!'

Jonah stared at her earnest crimson face. Then he tapped her gently on the nose. 'Sweetheart,' he said, 'wait until you're asked.'

Temporarily, she hated him. 'We'll have coffee in the sitting room,' she told him sniffily. What else was she to think he'd had in mind had they gone to Yourk House that weekend? Yet here he was making it seem as if she were some kind of female sex maniac!

The washing machine started creating again. Jonah picked up the tray and they were both glad to go to the sitting room. He waited until Lydie was seated, the coffee on a table by her side, and he took a seat nearby.

'So, what have you in mind?' she enquired, thawing a little, loving him too much to hate him for long.

'Anything you care for,' he replied. 'Take a drive, have lunch out, find a church fête—I might even win you a tin of baked beans on the tombola.'

He made her smile and, while she wondered how he knew about anything so simple and villagey as a church fête, she thawed completely. She knew he would never fall in love with her; she had seen the type of woman he was attracted to and, remembering the sophisticated blonde, Freya, he had been at the theatre with, Lydie knew better than to wish for the moon.

'I...' She hesitated, and just then, even though she knew she would guard with her life against him getting so much as a whiff of her feelings for him, she knew that she wanted his company. 'I'm not fit to be seen,' she replied. No way, other than with sunglasses to hide her red-rimmed eyes, was she going to any restaurant for lunch. 'If you're serious, bearing in mind you've tired of the hunt and that I represent no threat—to either your virtue...' he laughed, and she loved him some more '...or to your bachelorhood, I could fix us some lunch here.' Oh, heavens, how intimate that sounded!

'You said you weren't much of a cook?'

'I lied,' she answered. 'Though, since it wouldn't seem right to me to raid my great-aunt's pantry, anything we get from the village shop will probably be cooked already.'

Somehow, and Lydie could almost pinpoint it exactly, it seemed to her then as if their relationship, friendship, whatever it was, had changed. He seemed even more sensitive than he had previously been and, as they took a stroll up to the village store, Lydie felt she could talk to him about anything. Not that she had any secrets to keep; he probably knew more about her family finances than she did.

It was a fact that they seemed in harmony for once. Talking non-stop on occasions, about any subject that came up, and at other times not talking at all. They were eating lunch of oven heated frozen chicken and mushroom pie, with potatoes, broccoli and carrots, when Jonah asked her about her boyfriends. She did not wish to let the side down, so thought to admit to a few. 'There haven't been too many,' she replied.

'I'm to believe that?' He obviously didn't.

'It took me longer than most to get over the crippling shyness of adolescence.'

He smiled across at her. 'Which makes you a rather special person, Lydie Pearson. When you would have been about sixteen years old, and I came to your house to ask your father for a loan, you must have known why I was there and, despite your desperate shyness, you seemed to want to put me at my ease.'

'I asked you if you would like some tea.'

'You were charming,' he said, and her heart danced. 'What about Charlie?' Jonah asked in almost the same breath, and Lydie stared at him.

'What about Charlie?' she asked, for the moment mystified.

'You were going to give him the "big E",' Jonah reminded her.

'Oh!' she exclaimed, startled. 'I meant to ring him.' She had—to ask him how he'd fared with his office colleague, Rowena Fox.

'You forgot?' Jonah challenged.

She didn't want to fight with him. 'It isn't important.'

'You don't sound too involved?'

'How about you? Given that you're not hunting any more?'

'My last couple of—um—sorties—came to an abrupt end when the words "moving in" first crept into the conversation.'

Lydie laughed. 'That had you running scared.'

'Too right!' he grinned. 'Oh, Lydie, it's good to see you laugh.'

Jonah helped her with the dishes, and helped her through sad reflective moments too when, as happened through the day, the sadness of losing her great-aunt would unexpectedly well up and choke her.

'Your father sold the family business, I believe,' she said unceremoniously at one such moment. She knew Jonah would understand, but she just did not want to cry in front of him.

'The sale was completed four years after your father so very kindly backed my venture into fibre optics,' Jonah agreed, and, going on purely to get her over her sad moment, Lydie felt, 'It was fortunate that when I knew that another day spent in the retail business would drive me out of my mind, my brother, Rupert, showed a keen interest in entering the family firm.'

'You were able to leave and set up in business that went well?'

He nodded. 'Though I have to say that my father didn't take it too well.'

'He refused to back your fibre optic venture?'

Jonah paused, and she felt privileged when he confided, 'My father and I were at odds with each other for a while—I wouldn't ask him for money. In fact,' he went on, 'when later Rupert decided he wanted out of the business too, and my father started to consider the offers he'd many times had for his business and then decided to sell, I didn't expect to receive any money.'

'But you did,' Lydie said softly, knowing it was so.

'I should have known better. Whatever our differences, my father has always been fair with Rupert and me. Rupert received a quarter of the proceeds—so too did I.'

'And you at once paid my father back.'

'But only in money. I owed him more than that. Wilmot had faith in me when the money institutions were saying they'd gone as far as they could.'

They finished the dish-washing and putting everything away with Lydie realising that it was because of that faith her father had shown in him that Jonah had given her that cheque. 'I *will* pay you back—that money you gave me,' she told Jonah sincerely. And, while they were on the subject, 'Have you thought of anything yet? Other than my making monthly payments to you from my earnings?'

'Let's not talk about it today, Lydie,' he answered sensitively.

And she smiled at him, but felt he should know that her father did not take the matter lightly. 'While the debt is mine, I really want you to understand that my father is a most honourable man,' she told Jonah earnestly.

'I know,' he replied quietly.

But that did not seem enough. 'He would have sold the house, but…'

'He was ready to sell Beamhurst Court?' Jonah seemed very much surprised.

'It's all he has left to sell.'

'But it's been in your family for ever!'

'My father was desperate,' she stated. But, as Jonah had confided a little about his father, Lydie felt she could confide about her mother's role in the non-sale of Beamhurst Court. 'It hasn't come to selling yet. My mother is sticking out against selling—she's objecting most strongly.'

'Your mother loves Beamhurst Court as you do?'

'It's not so much that, I think,' Lydie confessed. 'She wants it for Oliver.'

'And does Oliver want it? I heard he was having some five star place built in the grounds of the Ward-Watson home?'

'Unless he drastically changes his opinions, he wouldn't touch Beamhurst with a bargepole,' Lydie answered, guessing that with Oliver and Madeline's plans general knowledge at the wedding, Jonah had picked up a snippet about the new house there. But Lydie was feeling strangely shy all at once. 'You'll be wanting to get off home now, I expect,' she said quickly, feeling very conscious that she had monopolised so much of his time and, while not wanting him to go, feeling guilty because of it.

But it seemed Jonah had nothing pressing that day to get back to. 'Don't give me hints, woman,' he teased. 'Tell me straight out.' She smiled, but could not find an answer. And he asked, 'Do you want to be on your own, Lydie?'

She shook her head. 'No,' she said.

'Then we'll go for a walk,' he decreed.

It was for the most part a silent walk, though Lydie did think to ask, 'What were you doing following me yesterday? I thought you'd be on your way to your Hertfordshire home.'

'I had business in your area. I anticipated you'd leave around six and thought we'd go in tandem—me leading the way in case you got lost. I was tucked in near the crossroads when you shot by. Do you want me to apologise again for being so swinish to you?'

She smiled at him and shook her head, just grateful to have him with her for this short time. They walked on, Jonah busy with his thoughts, and Lydie overcome with sadness on seeing the bench near the church where she and her great-aunt had sat on one of their evening strolls.

She felt saddened that she would never sit on that bench with Aunt Alice again. And, as other memories arrived, saddened that she would not again go with her to some Saturday afternoon function at the village hall. Then, lastly, a feeling of guilt came to trip Lydie up.

She and Jonah were on their way back to the house when a shaky kind of sigh took her, and Jonah caught a sympathetic hold of her hand. 'Bad moment?' he asked kindly.

'Guilt,' Lydie replied unthinkingly.

'All part of the territory when you lose someone you care for,' he assured her.

'Is it?'

He let go her hand and smiled down at her.
'Want to talk about it, Lydie?'

'Oh, you know. Generally I could have visited
her more than I did.'

'You stayed overnight with her Saturday,' he
reminded her quietly. 'And didn't you say you'd
seen her again only on Thursday?'

'I came over on Monday and stayed until
Thursday.' Lydie could feel herself going pink as
she remembered. She looked up and saw Jonah
was looking down at her—he couldn't help but
notice her embarrassed colour. She knew then that
she had some confessing to do. 'I've done a terrible thing,' she owned.

'Are you likely to go to jail for it?' he enquired
lightly.

'Hopefully not,' she answered, and then blurted
out, 'I can't stop telling lies. I never used to,' she
hurried on. 'Before I took that cheque from you
lies and my tongue were strangers. But ever since
I just seem to open my mouth and all these lies
pour out!'

'Oh, my word—should I worry?'

'I *have* involved you,' she admitted.

His tone did not change. 'Perhaps you'd better tell me what's been going on,' he suggested mildly.

Lydie thought for a moment, and then said, 'I had intended to come and see Aunt Alice on Tuesday last anyway—and that's where some of the guilt I feel comes in—I came on Monday instead. But only partly for Aunt Alice. More specifically, I came on Monday mainly because I was afraid if I stayed home yet more lies would come tumbling out. For the same reason I stayed on here with my great-aunt until Thursday.'

'Afraid to go home?'

'Something like that. I wanted to avoid my tongue running away with me.' Jonah was silent. He was waiting—and she did not want to tell him. But his very silence seemed to be compelling her to go on. 'I've told the most howling lies!' She paused—Jonah wasn't helping her out. 'On Monday. You know, when you rang. Well, I went to give my father your message, that you'd rung and wanted to speak with him, and before I could say more he was ready to sprint back to the house to take your call. Anyhow, I stopped him by saying you were going out of the country but that you'd talk with him next week.'

'So far you don't appear to have told any fresh lies,' Jonah commented dryly.

She was glad to feel a touch niggled with him, but the feeling did not last. How, after what she had done, dared she be in any way annoyed? 'Anyhow, my father suddenly looked so defeated, so at the end of his rope, so as if—as if he's thought himself to a standstill trying to find some solution, that I couldn't bear it. He was saying something about this could not go on, and looked so much as though he was worn to his roots and couldn't take another day of it, so—um...' Oh, grief. 'I couldn't take it, Jonah. I told him—that you had a proposition to put to him that you said would be the answer.'

She ran out of breath, and waited for Jonah's wrath to fall about her ears for her nerve. But, instead of being furious with her, he politely enquired, 'And what is this proposition, Lydie? Am I not entitled to know?'

Perhaps his wrath would have been better, she mused. 'I haven't worked anything out yet. I just wanted him to have some respite from it all. I thought that while you were out of the country, and until the two of you meet—which I can see now that you're going to have to—it might give him about a week of not worrying so much. Give his poor head a chance to get perhaps a little rest.'

'He *was* looking a little less stressed out last night than when I saw him last Saturday,' Jonah acknowledged. 'You'd better tell me word for word exactly what you said to him in my name.'

Lydie felt a bit pink about the ears again at that last bit. 'That's about it, I think,' she replied. 'A spark of life seemed to come to my father's eyes, and I found myself lying—I just couldn't seemed to stop—and telling him that you wouldn't say what your proposition was, but that whatever it was you were certain, if he agreed to it, that your proposition would be the answer to all his worries.'

'And he bought that?'

'He said he'd thought and thought but he couldn't see a way out of the hole he was in, but that if anyone could then you would be the one to do it.'

'And that was all?'

Lydie, having arrived back at her great-aunt's door without knowing it, thought hard. She shook her head. 'Dad asked if you wouldn't tell me more than that, and, while I couldn't regret having put hope back in his eyes, I started to worry that if he pressured me to say more I might end up telling him even more and bigger lies.'

'So you decided to make yourself scarce.'

'I came here,' Lydie agreed. And, as she knew she had to, said, 'I'm sorry, Jonah. I've behaved disgracefully. But my punishment will be that I must now go home and take that ray of hope from my father's eyes by confessing what an outrageous liar he has for a daughter.'

Whether Jonah accepted her apology she knew not, but he stood looking down at her for long moments, and she would loved to have known what he was thinking. Then, his expression still thoughtful, 'Don't confess anything just yet,' he instructed.

Her eyes widened. 'You've thought of something?' she enquired eagerly, getting used now to the way her heart misbehaved from time to time when she was with him. 'You've thought of some kind of proposition? Some kind of—?'

'Leave it with me,' Jonah cut in.

'You've thought…?'

'Something's filtering away inside the old grey matter,' was all that he would say.

'But…' She started to probe anyway, but could see he wasn't going to be drawn, no matter how much she pressed. So she had to let it go, but did ask, 'You're not mad at me?'

Jonah gave her a hint of a smile. 'Any lies you've told, Lydie, were not for yourself, but to try and make life more bearable for your father than it is just now.' She simply stared at him, marvelling at him understanding. Then he had done away with the subject, and was asking, 'Any chance of a cup of tea before I go?'

They went inside and Lydie made some tea, reflecting that she had never envisaged last Sunday that she would spend time with him this weekend in this way. Thoughts of her great-aunt were never very far away, however, her passing away so recent, and again Lydie thought sadly, if fondly, of her great-aunt.

'I'd better get going before I outstay my welcome,' Jonah said, finishing the last of his tea and getting to his feet. And while Lydie was wishing he would stay for ever, but starting to be positive he must have a date that night, she got up and went to the door with him. 'You've no objection if I attend Miss Gough's funeral?' he asked.

'You don't have to do that,' she said in a rush, already too much indebted to him.

'You ashamed of me?' he asked, his mouth quirking in that way that made her feel all gooey over him.

She shrugged to combat the feeling. 'You scrub up quite nicely,' she told him, and felt pretty wonderful about him when he laughed.

Though he was serious when, standing close to her, he looked down into her smiling green eyes and instructed, 'Try not to worry—I'll think of something.'

Mutely she stared up at him, then didn't know where the Dickens she was when, for all the world as though he could not help himself, Jonah took her in his arms—and kissed her!

The feel of his lips on hers in that oh, so gentle kiss turned her legs to water. She wanted to cling on to him, to return his kiss, to cling on to him for evermore and to never let go.

But jealousy, that stranger to her until now, that foul stranger that perched on her shoulder and from nowhere tormented her that Jonah would probably have his arms around some other woman that night, gave her no option but to push him away from her. 'Sweetheart,' he had said, 'wait until you're asked.'

'Sweetheart,' she said, finding her voice sounding incredibly stern when her legs felt about to collapse, 'I do trust you're not asking?'

For a moment Jonah looked as though he couldn't believe his hearing. Then he burst out laughing. 'You'll know when, Lydie, without having to ask,' he promised—and went.

Lydie closed the door, not knowing whether to laugh or cry. Her heart was still thundering in her ears as she returned to the sitting room and collapsed on to a chair. Jonah had kissed her! Jonah had kissed her, she marvelled. And she, idiot, had pushed him away!

CHAPTER SIX

HER great-aunt's funeral was an occasion Lydie was not looking forward to. But given that Oliver—who had never particularly got on with his mother's aunt—was on his honeymoon and did not attend, it passed quietly and in a dignified manner. Lydie had spotted that Jonah was there, but he did not presume to come and sit in the family pew.

He came over to her in the general standing around afterwards, though, and asked how she was. 'Fine,' she answered, and he was still next to her when her father walked over to them.

The two men shook hands. 'You'll come back to the house?' Wilmot Pearson asked Jonah.

To Lydie's surprise Jonah accepted. He was a busy man and Thursday was a work day. 'Perhaps I could see you at some convenient time after today?' Jonah suggested to him, and Lydie started to get all churned up inside. Plainly Jonah had put his thinking cap on and had come up with something.

'No disrespect to Miss Gough, but today would suit quite well,' her father replied, a further endorsement, if Lydie didn't know it, that her dear father was likely to have heart failure if he had to wait much longer to have a talk with Jonah.

'Whenever you say, Wilmot,' Jonah agreed.

'Until later,' her father said, and went on to talk to family members who, until Oliver's wedding not two weeks ago, he had not seen for some while.

'You've thought of something?' Lydie asked Jonah the moment her father was out of earshot.

'All in good time,' Jonah murmured, and Lydie knew at once she was going to get nothing more out of him.

To show her disgust she walked over to Muriel Butler, whom she just then noticed, and thanked her for attending.

'Such a sad day,' Muriel answered, and they chatted for a few minutes, then, deciding that Jonah couldn't leave her not knowing, Lydie went back to him. By then, though, he had been annexed by her beautiful cousin Kitty.

'I was just telling Jonah how I saw him at Oliver's wedding but you'd whisked him off somewhere before we could be introduced.'

Lydie had always envied her cousin her self-assured air, and wished some of it had brushed on to her. 'You've introduced yourself now, I hope?' She smiled, her manners holding up despite the green-eyed spears that were prodding. Jonah did not look to be at all put out that the beautiful, self-assured Kitty was batting her big brown eyes at him.

At that moment, however, a general move was made to where everyone had parked their cars. The cortège had left from Alice Gough's home, but the family, in the absence of her having close friends, were assembling back at Beamhurst Court. No matter what, on their uppers though they might be, Hilary Pearson was going to have things done properly.

'Want to drive back with me, Lydie?' Jonah asked as Kitty trotted off.

Lydie had come in the lead car with her parents, but it would suit her quite well to drive back to Beamhurst Court with Jonah. 'I'll just tell my father,' she accepted, but discovered that she did not have to tell her father anything. Somehow, and she rather thought she had no one to blame but herself, her parents seemed to believe that she and Jonah had something 'going'. Her father must have assumed she would be driving back with Jonah anyway, because he waved to them and turned and, with a hand on her mother's elbow, escorted his wife down the church path.

Much good did it do Lydie to drive with Jonah. 'What are you going to say to my father?' she asked as soon as they were in his car and moving.

'For the moment,' he replied carefully, 'that must be between your father and me.'

'Don't be mean!' she erupted. 'I've as much right...'

'Stamping your foot, Lydie?' Jonah mocked. But, perhaps bearing in mind that they had just come from her beloved aunt's funeral, 'I don't want you to be more upset—I just feel I have to speak to your father first.'

Not be more upset! Lydie fumed. 'You won't distress him? If I...'

'I hope not to distress him,' Jonah answered— and with that she had to be content.

But she watched. At her home, with her relatives assembled in the drawing room, Lydie watched. She chatted and looked after the more mature members of the family group, but the whole time she knew where Jonah was and where her father was.

She was talking to her mother's cousin when she saw her father look across to Jonah. Kitty had annexed him again but, whatever unspoken signal had passed between her father and Jonah, when a minute later her father left the drawing room she saw Jonah skilfully excuse himself from Kitty and, casually, he strolled from the drawing room too. She knew he would meet her father and they would go to his study.

They were gone for a half-hour. She knew because she had spent that half-hour in either looking to the drawing room door, watching for them to come back, or looking at her watch. What on earth were they talking about all this while?

With her insides churning, her heart seemed to somersault when, together, the two men dearest in the world to her came and stood in the drawing room doorway. She tried to read something, anything from their faces. Jonah's expression was telling her nothing. Her glance went quickly to her father. His expression was telling her little more other than that whatever proposition Jonah had put to him it had not depressed him. He looked more thoughtful than anything—though certainly not down. She started to hope.

Lydie was by then on the other side of the room from where she had been half an hour ago. She went to move across the room, but as she did so, without looking at her but just as if he had known from where he stood just exactly where she was, Jonah moved forward and blocked her way.

She halted, looked up, her glance moving worriedly from him to her father. She opened her mouth, but Jonah, taking a restraining hold of her arm spoke first. 'Let's go for a stroll, Lydie,' he said quietly.

She stared at him, her lovely green eyes still trying to read something in his expression. He was telling her nothing. She looked from him, looked around the room. Everyone seemed comfortable; no one was sitting alone staring into space.

'Yes,' she murmured, and was more churned up than ever. The only reason Jonah could be suggesting a stroll was so that he could tell her what she wanted to know: what the proposition was that he had put to her father.

They left the house and walked up the long drive. They went out through the gates. Jonah seemed to be more deep in thought than ready to let her know of his discussion—his half-hour discussion—with her parent in the study. She did not want to be again accused of 'stamping her foot' and, having learned that she was going to get nothing out of Jonah until he was good and ready, with more patience than he could know, she waited.

They were walking her favourite walk, and she waited until, having strolled down a picturesque lane, the air scented with honeysuckle, they left the lane and turned to where a five-barred gate led into a meadow. It was then that Lydie could wait no longer. She stopped walking; Jonah halted too.

'So?' she asked—a shade belligerently, she had to admit—and realised that the stresses of more than one kind that day were getting to her. 'What have you got to tell me?'

His reply was not at all what she had been expecting. And was in fact totally staggering when, turning to face her, he looked down into her eyes, and, after a moment, very clearly said, 'I've decided—it's time I married.'

Lydie wasn't sure her jaw did not drop. 'But—you don't want to marry,' she argued, feeling sick inside. But, rapidly getting herself together—this would never do—she forced a smile. 'Let me congratulate you, Jonah.' He was going to marry Freya, that lovely blonde creature! Though hadn't he said something about not seeing the blonde again after that theatre date?

'Thank you,' he accepted.

'You've obviously known the lady in question some while?' she fished.

'You could say that,' he replied, adding, when Lydie knew that it was nothing whatsoever to do with her, 'I hope you approve of my choice.'

She didn't; she wouldn't. In fact just then she was ready to stick pins in his choice! Somehow, though, when what she wanted to do was to run and hide herself away to get over this awful blow, Lydie managed to keep control; even her father was for the moment forgotten as she fought to mask that she was falling apart. 'Do I know her?' she asked casually. She was going to hate him if it *was* Freya.

Lydie had felt staggered before. But his answer this time was to shake her to her very foundations, when, looking nowhere but at her, 'You,' Jonah replied succinctly, 'are her.'

Lydie stared at him, disbelieving her ears. Then her jaw very definitely did drop open—it almost hit the ground. *'Me!'* she gasped, and, her eyes saucer wide, she just looked at him. 'Are you serious?'

'I wouldn't joke about something like this.'

'Y-you're saying you want to—marry me?' Was that squeaky voice hers?

'That's my plan,' he confirmed, set, determined, everything about him brooking no refusal.

Well, she'd soon see about that! Just because he had now decided it was time he married, he thought he'd have a pot-shot at her—well, could he think again! 'I'm not marrying you!' she told him in no uncertain fashion. Love him she might, but *really*!

'Yes, you are,' he countered, not a bit abashed.

'Give me one good reason why I should,' she challenged hostilely.

'I can think of fifty-five thousand reasons,' he returned coolly—and on that instant her hostility immediately evaporated.

A soft gasp of 'Oh!' escaped her as thoughts of her father rocketed in. 'You've...' Her voice failed her. 'This isn't the proposition you put to my father. It can't be.' It wasn't making sense. 'What sort of proposition would that be? To marry...' She ran out of steam; her brain seemed to have seized up.

Jonah came in to help her out. 'Let's put it this way. We both know that your father is a proud man, an honourable man. Now, you tell me—who would he rather owe money to? An acquaintance or a member—albeit a son-in-law—of his family? An outsider—or an insider?'

Lydie looked from him. She needed space, some time to think. Jonah had out of the blue just hit her with this notion that they marry to make him a member of her family, an insider, and thereby make that money all within the family.

'The debt is mine, not my father's,' was the poor best she could come up with.

'That's not the way he sees it,' Jonah replied. 'Nor will you be able to convince him any other way.'

Lydie knew that he was right, but, 'I can't marry you,' she insisted.

'Your father's peace of mind isn't worth it?'

'Oh, don't, Jonah!' she cried. 'Of course it is,' she said fretfully.

Jonah smiled kindly. 'I wish I could give you time to think about it, Lydie, but your father's expecting us to go back with happy smiles.'

'You've told him you were going to ask me?' She stared at him open-mouthed.

'He has a problem. He has thought and thought and cannot come up with a solution. To my mind this is the only solution for your father. For the moment we leave it that he owes a close family member a sum of money which, in time, I hope he will learn to live with. For my part I have no interest in having that money repaid.'

'But you don't want to be married. You said as much.'

'Can't a man change his mind?'

She supposed he could. 'But—why me?'

'Why not you? Ignoring the fact, for the moment, that by you marrying me I'm hoping to relieve the terrible stress and strain of a man I hold in the very highest regard, for myself I'd be getting a most beautiful wife. And, from what I've witnessed in today's sad circumstances alone, I shall also have myself a most admirable hostess.'

Some of her shock was starting to fade, but she still felt she needed time—time, space to think. She loved him, and now that the idea was settling in her head a little she could think of nothing she would rather do than marry him. But that did not make it right.

And from her father's viewpoint, yes, perhaps he would feel better able to live with owing that money to someone whom she did not doubt he would be pleased to look on as a son. But from her viewpoint—that still did not make it...

'Penny for them?' Jonah asked, and she realised she had been silent a long time and that he would not mind being let into her thoughts.

'How did my father take it? I mean, I can't see him simply saying "Oh, yes" when you mentioned you'd marry me to make him feel more comfortable about his debt.'

'I hope I wasn't that crude,' Jonah replied, going on, 'From what you've told me you have already given your father the impression that we're keen on each other. I let him think we had grown to love each other, and that I was asking his blessing that I should marry you.'

'Thank you for that,' Lydie said without thinking—she would rather her father thought she was marrying for love in preference to have him thinking she was marrying to make him feel better. Not that he would have stood for that anyway.

'Is that a yes?' Jonah asked quietly.

'No,' she said quickly, but could see how, from her thanking him for letting her father believe it would be a love match, Jonah would think she had agreed. 'That is,' she qualified, 'you've suddenly, in the space of three weeks, gone from running like blazes from the thought of marriage to deciding now that to marry would quite suit you? How do I know that you won't, three weeks into any marriage, just as suddenly ask for a divorce?'

'How can you talk of divorce when I've only just asked for your promise to marry me? Divorce,' he told her firmly, 'is not an option.'

Lydie still needed time, though could quite well see that if Jonah had told her father he was about to propose to her then her father, having noticed their absence, was going to think she had turned Jonah down should they return with nothing to announce. Which in turn would send him tumbling straight down into a pit of stress and depression again.

'Would it—um—this marriage—would it be a n-name only affair?' she asked, embarrassed, but needing to have a few answers now.

'I'm family-minded,' Jonah replied. 'I'm afraid we'd have to do what we have to do to produce a few offspring.'

Oh, heavens! 'Um,' she mumbled, and, more to get herself over some hot-all-over moments than anything, abruptly asked, 'What if—supposing—we find the money?' She was starting to feel confused. And no wonder! But remembering— was it only last Friday?—the way he had aggressively taken exception at the thought of being cheated—'No one cheats on me—*ever*,' he had said—'Supposing you and I were engaged and, and we found we could pay back the money. I'd be cheating you to marry you then—and you wouldn't like that.'

'You're wriggling, Lydie,' Jonah accused, plainly knowing as well as she that she and her father hadn't a hope in Hades of finding fifty-five thousand pounds and paying him back. 'And you'd have to find it pretty quickly.'

'I would?' She stared at him.

He nodded. 'Having decided it's time I married, I can't see any reason to wait.'

Lydie looked at him helplessly. She guessed that was part and parcel of the man—decide upon something, decision made, expedite it. But this wasn't business, this was her future, his future, and while as more shock receded she knew that

she could not think of anything she would rather
do than be his wife, to see him most every day—
it still did not seem right.

'You're sure you want to be married?' she
questioned.

'Totally sure.'

'And I'm—''it''—?'

'Don't sell yourself short, Lydie. You're a little
bit gorgeous.'

Her heart fluttered. 'I'm trying to be serious
here,' she told him sternly.

'You think I'm not?'

'What the alternative?' she asked. 'From my
father's point of view, I mean. What's the alternative if I don't marry you?'

Jonah shrugged. 'The money, as your father
sees it, will still be his debt. When I spoke with
him in his study a while ago, and acquainted him
with my plans, I saw that spark of hope in him
grow and grow the more we talked. I even felt as
we left his study that there was a bit of a spring
in his step that hadn't been there before,' Jonah
added, then asked quite simply, 'I've made my
decision, Lydie, may I now hear yours?'

She needed more time, only there wasn't more
time. Her father would be watching for them to
come back, would be searching their faces. Could
she bear to see that ray of hope die from his eyes?

Could she bear to see that hurt, that stress return to his eyes? As her father had said, he had thought and thought and could find no solution. He had great trust in Jonah and had said that if anyone could think up a way Jonah would be the one to do it. Well, he had, and, while it was true it might not be the proposition her father had hoped for, he would as the days went by, learn to live with the fact that his debt was not to a man he himself had once helped, but to his daughter's husband.

Oh, grief. Husband—Jonah! Her legs threatened to give way at the thought. She turned and placed a seemingly casual hand on the top of the five-barred gate, gripping it hard. Then, decision made, she turned back to him.

She looked up into his wonderful blue eyes and took a long steadying breath. 'It seems a bit formal to shake hands on—um—my promise,' she began, 'but I don't think I'm ready for k-kisses just yet.'

Jonah stared down at her for long moments, then raised a hand and brushed a stray something or other out of her hair. 'Your word is good enough for me, Lydie,' he said quietly. And then, oddly, seemed to draw a steadying breath himself at her acceptance of his marriage proposal. But Lydie knew that it was just her imagination gone wild—and no wonder—because his voice was totally matter of fact when, taking a step away from the gate, he suggested, 'We'd better get back.'

Lydie could only agree. Her father would be waiting, watching for their return. She fell into step with Jonah, but they were walking back up the drive when she thought of the sadness of the day, and hurriedly asked, 'We don't have to announce it—our engagement—straight away, do we?'

'It doesn't seem entirely appropriate to announce it generally today,' he agreed.

'Thank you for understanding,' she said softly.

And he looked at her and smiled. 'We'll be all right together, Lydie, trust me,' he said. And she did, and started to feel more on an even keel. 'We'll tell your parents when everyone has gone,' he decided, then seemed to realise that there was a partnership going on here, and added, 'If that's all right with you?'

Lydie had an idea he'd do as he pleased even if it wasn't all right with her, but, since he was going through the motions, 'Fine,' she agreed. Then they were at the steps of Beamhurst Court and her father, who had obviously been on the fidget, strolled, as if casually, out to meet them. 'I've—er—been showing Jonah my favourite walk,' Lydie said, and, as both her father and Jonah looked down at her, for no reason she blushed. Her father looked delighted. 'Can Jonah stay to dinner?' she heard herself blurting out.

'I think that can be arranged,' Wilmot Pearson answered, and for the first time since she had come home from Donna in Norfolk, Lydie actually saw her father grin. She knew then that to agree to marry Jonah had been the right decision. Already her father was starting to get back to being the man he used to be! It seemed incredible that, just to know that Jonah was to be his son-in-law—she would hardly have invited Jonah to dinner if she had turned him down—her father should at once be on the way to being his former self. But, remembering his grin—there were no two ways about it.

Gradually all the relatives trickled away, Kitty being one of the last to leave. Lydie would have quite liked to tell her cousin that the man she was drooling over was, as of today, affianced. But there was an order to these matters, and her parents had to be informed first.

Though, when she'd decided to go upstairs to change out of her mourning clothes, Lydie was on the staircase when she observed that Jonah and her father seemed to making for the study again. In all probability, she realised, Jonah was telling her father she had accepted him.

As, over dinner, she learned was true. Only her mother seemed unaware of what had taken place, and looked at her husband askance when he left the table and came back with a bottle of chilled champagne.

'How do you feel about gaining a son?' he asked her. And, with Hilary Pearson looking as much bemused by this suddenly playful change in the dour husband she had known of late as by what he said, 'Jonah has asked Lydie to marry him,' he added. 'And Lydie, I believe, has accepted.'

'Lydie's accepted...' her mother gasped. 'You're going to marry...'

Loving someone meant that no one was going to say anything against that someone, Lydie at once discovered, even if that someone was more than well able to take care of himself. And, 'Is it such a surprise, Mother?' she could not refrain from butting in.

Her mother recovered well. 'I'm very happy for you both,' she unbent sufficiently to say.

But was not so very happy when, a champagne toast drunk, Jonah let it be known that he was keen to marry as soon as possible.

'These things take an age to organize. A year at least,' his future mother-in-law let him know.

Jonah considered her answer, but not for very long. 'It looks like an elopement, Lydie,' he commented.

'Oh, no! Certainly not!' Hilary Pearson fired shortly. Jonah was unmoved. 'Six months?' she reconsidered.

'Six weeks at the very latest,' Jonah said firmly, and while Lydie was thinking, Six weeks! Grief—six short weeks! Jonah wanted them to be married before the next six weeks were out, he was battering down her mother's defences by stating, 'My mother would love to liaise with you to give a helping hand.' He did not need to say anything more.

'I'm quite sure I shall be able to manage,' Hilary Pearson assured him.

Later, as Lydie suspected was expected of her, she went out with Jonah to his car. 'Six weeks doesn't seem very long,' she suggested tentatively.

'I don't want to wait that long, but I appreciate your mother's point of view,' Jonah replied, adding with a smile in his voice, 'Some board of directors missed a gem when they didn't snap your mother up.'

After the tensions of the day it was good to be able to find a light spontaneous laugh. 'Would your mother really have helped out?' she asked a moment later.

'Try keeping her away!' They reached his car but, while he opened up the driver's door, he did not immediately get into the driving seat. Instead he bent inside and extracted something. It was a small box. He opened it and took out the most beautiful diamond and emerald engagement ring. 'Shall we see if it fits?'

'You've had this all day!' Incredulous, Lydie stood in the brilliance of the security lights and just stared at it. 'Oh, Jonah,' she whispered, her heart all his that, this day of her great-aunt's funeral, he had sensitively not given her his ring until now. He slid the ring home on her engagement finger.

'Come here,' he said softly, and gathered her in his arms. But, perhaps recalling that she was not ready for his kisses just yet, he did not kiss her, but just sealed the giving of his engagement ring to her, and Lydie accepting, by holding her close for long moments. Then he was putting her away from him, and preparing to get into his car. 'My folks are going to want to meet you. We'll have dinner with them. Tomorrow?'

Oh, crumbs! He was serious, then? Although with his ring new, strange on her finger, she rather thought she knew that. 'I'll—er—look forward to it,' she replied politely.

'You're going to have to stop telling lies, Lydie,' Jonah said, but she was pleased to see as he got into his car that he was smiling.

Lydie was a long time getting to sleep that night. Stark reality that hadn't until she was alone had time to settle was there in ample supply. Had it really happened? Was she truly engaged to marry Jonah Marriott? Her fingers went to her engagement ring. It was not a dream. She *was* engaged to marry the man whom she loved with everything that was in her.

And yet—it still didn't seem right. But if she said now that she would not marry him it would mean she would have to go to her father and confess her lies, confess that Jonah had had no proposition to put to him when she had told her father that he had. And, even worse from her father's pride point of view, she would have to admit that she had agreed to marry Jonah solely because he had suggested her father would feel better if his debt was to family and not outsiders.

Lydie knew then that she would go through with this marriage to Jonah. Her father, let alone his pride, had suffered enough. Yet Lydie also knew that she wanted to be married for herself alone. She wanted Jonah to marry her for her, and not because he had decided it was time to marry and saw marriage to her as fitting in nicely with easing the cares of a man he respected. A man Jonah respected so well that he, having repaid his own debt, still believed he owed a lot of his success to.

The trouble was, she loved Jonah so much; but not a word of love had he spoken to her. Hang it, they hadn't even kissed! Not engagement kissed. Though, remembering the day they had spent together last Saturday, and how he had kissed her on parting, thinking about it, Lydie had to be glad he had not kissed her today. Her legs had been ready to fold when his lips had touched hers the last time. How would she have reacted today to the feel of his lips when still in shock from the unexpectedness of his proposal?

Lydie finally fell asleep glad she had six weeks in which to grow used to the idea of marrying Jonah. Would six weeks be enough?

They dined with his parents and his brother the following evening. Both Jonah's father and mother were charming, his brother a bit like her own brother in personality, and all three seemed absolutely delighted that Jonah had at last chosen his bride.

Any chance of the next six weeks gliding smoothly by, however, were doomed to failure when the two prospective mothers-in-law met. Lydie's mother wanted matters arranged one way; Jonah's mother wanted to help—her way. Trying to keep the peace between the two of them was running Lydie ragged.

As luck would have it there was just one 'slot' available in her local church on the day Lydie and Jonah had decided upon. Choristers were booked, bell ringers engaged and, after an extensive search, one of the best photographers. Limousines were chartered, caterers given detailed instructions, florists visited, designs chosen and outfits ordered.

Lydie could not believe her mother was so enthusiastically spending money they had not got, and protested vehemently again and again as the cost of the wedding rose higher and higher. 'Really, Mother, it's got to stop!' she exclaimed more than once.

'Don't be tiresome!' was her mother's response. 'You're our only daughter. Besides, I'm not going to let that Mrs Marriott think we're paupers!'

That Mrs Marriott! They'd obviously had a sharp exchange of views. 'But we haven't got this kind of money!'

'Oh, for goodness' sake! You're marrying a man worth a mint! Do you think your father and

I would let you go to him in anything but the very best?'

Matters might have been helped had Jonah been around for Lydie to talk to. But in his endeavours to get all his work cleared, so they could fly to a secluded sun-soaked island for a couple of months, he was here, there and everywhere. More often than not he was out of the country. Lydie rarely saw him.

He telephoned regularly, though, but she hardly felt she could complain about her lot when, although she was kept busy, he was so much busier. So Lydie silently got on with obeying her mother's 'get this, get that, ring here, ring there' instructions, her 'Don't forget your dress fitting,' and 'No, no, no, you cannot have lisianthus in your wedding bouquet,' and 'Do try and contact Kitty—she's the most tiresome child.' That 'child' was twenty-six and was to be one of Lydie's four bridesmaids because 'You cannot have just Donna!' her mother had exclaimed, horrified.

'Who's going to pay for all this?' Lydie wanted to know, starting to think that Jonah's hint of an elopement was the much better plan. Her question was brushed aside while her mother thought of someone else she really must send an invitation to.

Lydie was glad to get out of the house and drive to her dear great-aunt's home. It was not the happiest task to dispose of her belongings, but at least Lydie had peace and quiet and space to think her own thoughts.

She sighed as she folded away the last of her great-aunt's clothes. It was all getting to be just too much. To avoid further battles with her mother she had agreed to four attendants—three cousins and Donna. And since she had agreed, and because her cousin Kitty was beautiful, and pride decreed that Jonah should not think she was afraid of the competition, Kitty was to be one of them. Her other two cousins, Emilia and Gaynor, were extremely pretty too, as also was Donna.

Lydie waited for the furniture people to come and collect her great-aunt's bits and pieces and then took the keys and a memento of a piece of fine porcelain next door to Muriel Butler. Muriel had said she would quite like to have Miss Gough's cooker, and would have the keys to enable her to let the service men in to cut off the gas supply prior to reconnecting the cooker in her own home.

'I'll hand the keys in to the council too, if you like,' Muriel offered. 'It will save you having to come back to collect them from me. I've got to go in to pay my rent, and they won't care who hands them in so long as they've got them.'

Lydie had grown to like Muriel, who had always been kind and friendly to her great-aunt. Lydie would not have minded returning—Aunt Alice's home had been a kind of bolthole when things got too stressed at home—but she accepted Muriel's offer.

Lydie then went home to find her father hiding in the summer house. Love her mother as he dearly did, it seemed there were times when he preferred his own company.

'Have you been in yet?'

Lydie shook her head. 'I thought I spotted a figure lurking this way,' she replied, astounded at the change in him since Jonah had told him he wanted to marry her. Talk about bright-eyed and bushy-tailed! Even the expense of her wedding hadn't dimmed that new sharper air about him.

'Um—your dear mother has a lot on her mind. It—er—might be an idea for you to go in quietly.' From that Lydie knew she was in trouble over something. She had an idea what it was.

Her mother was waiting for her. 'Did you ring the florists and countermand my instructions?' she demanded the moment Lydie went in.

'I didn't ring; I called in when I was passing.'

'Deliberately passing! You *know* we agreed we wanted lilies for your bouquet, and—'

'I'm sorry, Mother,' Lydie cut in. Against her better judgement and for the sake of peace, albeit reluctantly, she'd had to go along with everything her mother had decreed must be. But on the issue of her bouquet Lydie had dug her heels in. 'It was *you* who wanted lilies in my bouquet.'

'Better than the red roses Grace Marriott suggested,' Hilary Pearson sniffed.

'I'd prefer to have pink and white lisianthus,' Lydie said, even as she said it wondering why she was being so stubborn.

'I'll have to change everything now!' her mother grumbled. 'The church flowers, the flowers in the marquee. The—'

'Lilies will be lovely,' Lydie said gently, 'everywhere else.'

'Grace Marriott phoned.' Thankfully Hilary Pearson went off on another tack. 'She's thought of someone else she wants to invite!' she complained, when she was adding to the list herself all the time. Grace Marriott's phone call was the subject of her mother's conversation, or rather Grace Marriott's interference was, for the next ten minutes. So that when, mid-way through being harangued about her future mother-in-law's misdeeds, the telephone rang and her mother broke

off to order, 'You answer it. I'm much too busy,'
Lydie was heartily glad to escape. Her mother
went in search of Mrs Ross; Lydie went to answer
the phone. It was Jonah!

'Where are you?' Lydie wanted to know.

'You sound as though you need me?' Was that
hope she heard in his voice? Fat chance!

'I've managed quite well with not seeing you
for more than the briefest occasion,' she answered
coolly, to hide that she felt all trembly inside from
hearing him. Heaven alone only knew how she'd
feel when she was standing beside him, marrying
him!

'You're saying you've missed me?'

'I hardly know you!' she retorted pithily. It was
a fact. She had seen him so rarely since their engagement he had become a stranger.

'We'll make up for that on our honeymoon,'
he said, to shatter any small amount of calm she
might have found. 'What's wrong?' he asked.

Lydie wanted to deny that anything was wrong,
but found she was answering truthfully. 'I suppose, not to put too fine a point on it, I'm feeling
the pressure.'

'About the wedding?'

'To be blunt, between them your mother and
my mother and what I should want and what they

don't want—and they're not agreeing about that anyway—are driving me potty.'

'As bad as that?'

She had to laugh. 'Not really,' she said, ready to apologise for her bad humour. 'I just wouldn't mind having your job for a while, where I could fly away and leave all this behind.'

'Are you propositioning me?'

She blinked. 'Pardon?'

'Forgive me. I thought you were suggesting we hid away at Yourk House this weekend.'

'You're free this weekend?' she queried, her heart starting to thunder. 'You've been so busy…'

'Perhaps we should spend a little time this side of marriage in getting to know each other.'

The idea had instant appeal. Not only would she be away from her mother's constant supply of something else to stress her out about, but she would be with Jonah. 'Er—are *you* propositioning me?' she asked him in turn. But, nervous suddenly, she went on hurriedly, 'I—um—that is, later, I know…'

'Calm down, Lydie,' Jonah instructed, a touch of humour in his voice. 'What are you trying to say?'

She swallowed down her agitation. This was ridiculous. For heaven's sake, she was marrying the man in two weeks' time! 'B-basically,' she began chokily, 'what I'm trying to say is that I'm—er—not read to c-commit…'

There was a pause. Then Jonah was asking, 'As in—sleep with me?'

'That's about it.'

Another moment of silence followed, then, 'We could have a non-committed weekend at Yourk House?' he suggested.

Oh, yes. She loved him so. Ached so just to see him. 'I'd have my own room?' Why was she prevaricating? For goodness' sake, he'd be telling her to forget it any minute now!

'Non-committed goes hand in hand with you having your own room,' Jonah assured her.

'Oh, Jonah, am I being difficult?' She all at once felt dreadful. 'I'm sorry. You're probably stressed out too!' He said nothing, and she went rushing on, 'Bearing in mind what's between us, I'd like to be friends with you—if we can.'

She could almost see him smile as he rolled the words, 'Friends and lovers,' around on his tongue. And, while her heart was jumping around like a wild thing, 'But not the two together this week-end,' he said softly. 'Do you know, Lydie, I would be honoured to be your friend.'

Her backbone was ready to melt. 'Shall I see you at Yourk House on Saturday?' she asked, striving her hardest to be sensible.

'I'll call for you at your place around six on Friday,' Jonah decided, and, with nothing more to agree on, 'Till then,' he said, and rang off.

And Lydie came away from the phone in something of a daze. It seemed a positive age since she had last seen Jonah, but she was gong to spend the whole weekend with him—which they would use in getting to know each other. She couldn't wait. She absolutely hungered for a sight of him. She loved him so much.

CHAPTER SEVEN

FRIDAY could not come round fast enough, though her mother was not at all pleased that Lydie would not be at home that weekend. 'I just don't know how you can think of going away when there's such a lot still to be done!' Hilary Pearson complained.

Lydie did not want to argue. 'Mother you're such a brilliant organiser,' she replied, which was only the truth. 'You're so far in advance, my being away for the weekend won't make a scrap of difference.'

'There's you wedding dress…'

'I'm collecting it next Wednesday.' And, beating her mother to it, 'And I've arranged with Kitty, Emilia and Gaynor to see them on Thursday about their fittings.'

'Donna…'

'And I'm taking Donna'a dress with me when I go to see her.'

'What if…?'

'And it shouldn't need altering. Donna has spoken personally to the fitter over the phone.'

'It's a pity she can't leave those children for a day to come with you and your cousins on Thursday,' Hilary Pearson said sniffily.

Lydie was ready and waiting and eager to be away when Jonah called for her on Friday. She opened the door to him and saw him standing there tall, broad shouldered, saying nothing but just looking back at her with those fantastic blue eyes. For several speechless seconds while her insides went all peculiar all she was capable of doing was just staring at him. Was she actually marrying this fabulous all-male man two weeks tomorrow? Lydie looked from him and stepped back. 'My parents are out,' she excused them not being there to say hello, 'but I'm all ready.'

Gradually over the drive to Yourk House Lydie started to unwind. She rather thought Jonah had a lot to do with that. 'Still stressed out?' he asked pleasantly as they motored on.

'I'm sorry about that,' she apologised. 'Compared with what you must cope with every day, my getting in a state—stamping my foot, you'd call it—because my mother wants me to carry a bouquet of lilies when I want to carry lisianthus seems quite ridiculous.'

'No, it doesn't,' he denied. 'You're the bride. If you want to carry a posy of dandelions nobody should stop you.' She laughed. She loved him. 'What *are* you carrying?' he asked.

'Lisianthus,' she answered.

'Did I ever tell you that lisianthus are my favourite flowers?'

Lydie laughed again. Lying hound! 'You don't even know what they look like!' she accused.

Yourk House was a lovely old house. It was set in its own grounds and did not appear to have a near neighbour. Lydie stood on the drive with him, and he glanced down at her. 'Come inside and I'll show you around—then you can tell me if you think you could be happy here.'

Lydie knew as soon as she walked through the door that she could be. The house seemed to have a feel about it. It welcomed her. 'We'll be living here after…?'

'When we're married,' he agreed, and dropped their weekend bags down by the bottom of the wide and elegant staircase while he showed her round the downstairs rooms.

Yourk House was not as old as her present home, nor did it have as many rooms as Beamhurst Court, but what it lacked in age and size it made up for in style and comfort.

Upstairs there were five bedrooms and adjoining facilities, and they looked at each bedroom in turn. 'This is the one I thought you'd like this weekend,' Jonah said, opening the door to a large, high-ceilinged airy room.

'It's lovely,' she murmured, and went in, admiring the four-poster bed and the charming furniture. She went over to the window and looked out. It was peaceful and tranquil, and she loved it.

Leaving that room, Jonah took her to see his bedroom, the master bedroom. And she knew that, when they returned from honeymoon, this would be her bedroom too. She would share this bedroom with Jonah. Her mouth went dry and she went to one of the windows in the room. She felt then that she should tell him that she had never slept with a man before—but her throat seemed too locked to tell him anything.

She knew he had come to stand beside her, but when he placed a casual arm about her shoulder, her thoughts just seemed to blank off. 'You're trembling!' She heard his voice somewhere above her head. 'Oh, my—' He broke off, and turned her to face him. She looked up at him; his expression was serious. 'You're—not afraid of me, Lydie?' he asked.

She immediately shook her head. 'No,' she answered truthfully. 'I'm not afraid of you at all.' She smiled at him, he seemed a shade worried and she didn't want that. 'What I am—and I can hardly believe it myself—is shy, I think. I thought I'd grown out of that long since, but...'

Her voice faded when Jonah took her in his arms and held her close up to him. Instinctively she placed her head on his chest, and he held her like that for long wonderful minutes. 'We'll be all right together,' he assured her. 'We've barely seen one another since we became engaged, and we didn't see so much of each other before then.' He paused, and then suggested, 'We'll make up for that this weekend.'

'Agreed,' she said, and, looking up, she smiled, and because she loved him, so as he looked down she stretched up and kissed him, not passionately, but a kiss that was perhaps just a little more than 'friends'. His arms tightened about her.

She pulled back. 'W-was that all right?' she asked shakily.

He smiled. 'Very all right,' he answered, and she started to wonder what on earth had got into her—and stepped back. 'Would you like to look around on your own while I shower and get out of my work clothes?' he suggested. 'Then we'll go out and eat.'

Lydie awoke early on Saturday morning in the room Jonah had shown her to. She lay there thinking of him and marvelling at how well they had got on with each other last night. She had not thought it possible to love him more than she had, but with each new facet she learned of him she fell yet deeper in love with him. He had been a charming dinner companion.

Thinking of the previous evening reminded her that, at some point in one of their many conversations that had rambled all over the place, he had last night, in some throwaway kind of remark, mentioned that nobody had brought him an early-morning cup of tea in bed since the day he had left home for university.

Lydie was out of bed in a flash, pausing for a moment to consider getting showered and dressed first, but then fearing that by then Jonah might be up and about. She tied her cotton wrap about her and tiptoed down the stairs.

A short while later, tea tray in hand, she was coming back up the stairs but was by then having second thoughts. She couldn't do it. It would be like invading his privacy. But why shouldn't she? It would make him smile, and anyway…

In the end, having dithered outside his door for long hesitating seconds, Lydie knocked lightly on his door and went in. 'Lydie!' he exclaimed, awake and starting to sit up. He seemed genuinely pleased to see her.

'Your tea, sir,' she said, and he too remembered their conversation, and grinned.

'Where's yours?' he wanted to know.

'I left it in the kitchen.'

Lydie went over to him, and as he sat there she saw from his broad naked chest that he seemed to favour sleeping in the raw—his top half anyway, and she didn't want to know about anything else. She averted her gaze and placed the tray on his bedside table.

She would have hurried away then, only he caught a light hold of her wrist. 'Come and talk to me,' he urged.

'I...' She looked into his wonderful eyes. 'What do you want to talk about?'

'Anything,' he replied, and moved over to make room. 'Sit here and—' his mouth quirked upwards '—naturally in a non-committed way, let's get—intimate.'

That word 'intimate' shook her a little, but any implication she might have been wary of was negated by his use, in the same sentence, of those words 'non-committed'. So she took that step needed to bring her against the bed.

'Here,' he said, holding out his right arm.

Lydie would have chosen to sit facing him, her feet on the floor, but this was the man she loved, for heaven's sake, and in no time she had disposed of her slippers and was sitting on top of the bed covers with Jonah's right arm about her shoulders. And—it was bliss.

Though with regard to talking about anything, feeling the warmth of his arm about her through the thinness of her light wrap, she could think of nothing else, and certainly nothing to say.

That was until, 'What pretty toes you have,' Jonah observed.

She looked at her pale delicate feet, which looked pretty normal to her. 'Thank you kindly,' she said, and laughed, and commented, 'Peculiar things, feet,' and laughed again at the absurdity of her answer, and was ready to collapse when he dropped a light kiss on her hair—as if he cared for her. 'Do you l-like me?' she asked in a rush, and immediately apologized. 'I'm sorry. I shouldn't have asked that.'

'Of course you should. I'd like to think we could talk about anything at all without embar-rassment.' She heard a smile creep into his voice as he went on to ask, 'And would I permanently marry myself to someone I actually *dis*liked?'

'That—wouldn't be sensible,' she murmured, striving her best to be sensible herself then and there, when his head came nearer, touched hers, and they sat, he under the covers from the waist down, she on top of the covers, with their heads one against the other. 'Er—what shall we do today?' she asked, about the only practical thing she could find floating around in her intellect just then.

'I've made arrangements for us to go and select our wedding rings,' he answered, causing her heart, which hadn't seemed to act normally for some while now, to start leaping about again.

'*Our* wedding rings?' she repeated. 'You're having a wedding ring as well?'

'If you're going to wear a marriage band, it seems only fair that I should,' he answered, and suddenly, after all the weeks of preparation that had been going on, only then did any of it all at once start to feel real.

Lydie pulled a little away from him, tense suddenly, half turning so she could see into his face. 'It's really going to happen, isn't it?'

'Our marriage?' She nodded, her eyes wide as she looked at him. He could, she supposed, have reminded her toughly of her father's despair if their marriage did not go ahead. But he didn't get tough, he instead smiled, and told her, 'Your future mother-in-law and my future mother-in-law will give us hell if it doesn't.'

Lydie had to smile, her tension instantly vanishing. She looked at him, loved him—and knew that this just would not do. 'I'd better go,' she said quickly, and would have manoeuvred herself off the bed—only Jonah took a hold of her hand and held her there.

She gave him a questioning glance. 'There's no hurry, sweetheart,' he murmured lightly, 'but how about we make a start by greeting each day—with a kiss?'

Lydie felt colour flare to her face. He was right, of course. Soon they would be man and wife, in every respect, maybe it was time to break down a few of those shyness barriers, and to skirt the edges of a more intimate relationship.

She looked at him. 'I'd like to,' she mumbled.

'Still lying, Lydie?'

'I'm never going to lie to you again,' she promised solemnly. 'But...' She was starting to tremble; she was wearing next to nothing. It was a new situation. 'I'm a bit nervous, I think,' she confessed. She had kissed him yesterday, but he had been dressed then, and today, now, this minute, he was wearing next to nothing too. It was a new situation and she felt too all over the place. 'Could you do it? The kissing, I mean.'

He stared at her for long moments, then, as if feeling her trembling and not wanting her nervous of him, he gently gathered her in his arms. 'You'll be safe with me, Lydie,' he breathed against her mouth, 'I'll never harm you.'

Oh, Jonah. Their lips met in such a gentle kiss she could have cried from the tenderness of it. She felt quite mesmerised when it ended, and looked deep into his eyes—until she suddenly became aware that her hands were on his hair strewn naked chest, her fingers touching his nipples.

'Oh!' she cried in consternation.

Jonah stared at her, comprehension dawning about what that 'oh' had been all about. 'You haven't had many lovers, have you, Lydie?'

Intimate? They were supposed to be getting to know each other—but she still couldn't tell him of her lack of knowledge in the lover department. 'I'm going,' she said, and leapt from the bed to hurry back to her own room.

She showered and got dressed feeling very much mixed up. Perhaps it was only natural that she should feel a shyness, a reserve, with the man she was going to marry. Theirs wasn't a normal kind of courtship, she knew. But perhaps in the getting to know each other field in normal courtships everyone found there were barriers to be dismantled, piece by piece. Then she remembered that wonderful kiss of not so long ago, and everything else faded from her mind.

They had a toast and coffee breakfast, and Lydie was glad to find Jonah's manner was the same as it had ever been. He was super to be with and she enjoyed every moment of sitting beside him as they motored into town.

They chose matching plain gold rings, and, Jonah taking charge of both rings, they left the jewellers and drove back to Yourk House. Lydie made them a sandwich lunch while Jonah checked the computer in his study for mail.

'I'll show you around the village,' he suggested after lunch, and they walked and talked and talked and walked, and Lydie's heart was so full she just wanted to hold and hold him. Theirs might not be a normal kind of courtship, or a courtship at all, but Jonah seemed to effortlessly be making an effort for them to start off on the right footing.

They dined out again that night. Jonah had a part-time live-out housekeeper who saw to it that Yourk House was kept up to the mark. 'Mrs Allen would have come in this weekend, but I thought we'd manage fine by ourselves,' Jonah confided, going on, 'Doubtless you'll want to organise household matters your own way when we return from our honeymoon. I'm sure Mrs Allen will be pleased to work to suit you.'

'From what I can see, Mrs Allen is doing a first-class job without any input from me. But I'll be glad to talk matters over with her,' Lydie replied, inwardly thanking him for trying to make the transition from daughter of one house to mistress of another smooth for her.

They returned to Yourk House after dinner, Lydie refusing the offer of coffee or any other beverage but offering to make coffee for Jonah if he fancied a cup. He shook his head. 'How are you feeling now?' he asked, once they were relaxing in his drawing room. 'You were a little strung up when I called for you yesterday.'

'It's amazing what a little over twenty-four hours can do,' she replied. 'I must have needed to get away for a short while.' She smiled across at him. 'If I get to feel any more relaxed, I'll fall over.' Jonah smiled too, his glance on her mouth, moving to her eyes, then back down to her lips again. Then Lydie was recalling the way he'd checked his mail in his study before lunch. 'Is there some work you should be doing? Don't let me stop...'

'You're trying to get rid of me,' he accused.

'Not at all!' she answered, but, having enjoyed being with him so much, she started to feel guilty about having monopolised so much of his time. 'I think I'll make tracks for bed,' she decided, and wished she'd kept her mouth shut when he did not argue.

She got to her feet, and Jonah followed suit, walking with her to the door. When he stopped at the door but instead of opening it just stood looking down at her, so Lydie realised that because this weekend together had brought them closer, they were now 'kissing fiancés'.

'Er—goodnight,' she said, and took a step nearer to him, her heart drumming that new beat. She raised her face to his, and he bent, and he kissed her.

'Goodnight,' he answered gravely, and abruptly opened the door for her to go through.

Lydie took another shower before getting into her nightdress and climbing into the four-poster. She and Jonah would be all right, wouldn't they? He was kind, considerate and, while he did not love her—did love matter? And if it did matter that he would never love her, what then? She would still have to marry him. For her father, if not for herself, she would have to marry Jonah.

She fell asleep knowing that above all else, when she and Jonah were married, she must guard against him learning of the love she had for him. Perhaps, given time, Jonah might come to care a little for her, but, remembering where his tastes lay—Freya whatever-her-name-was, for one— Lydie didn't hold out much hope. He was happy to choose someone unsophisticated to be the mother of his children, but when it came to play-mates women like Freya would win every time.

Having gone to sleep feeling not all that happy with her thoughts, nor with matters she could do nothing about, Lydie awoke with a start to find that it was morning, and that Jonah was in her room and had just placed a cup of tea down in her bedside table.

Instantly the sun came out for her and she struggled to sit up. 'I thought you liked to lie in on a Sunday morning!' she exclaimed, and felt at once all fluttering inside when Jonah bent down and, his fingers scorching her skin, casually put her slipped shoulder strap back in place.

'You remembered.' He grinned. 'I thought I should return yesterday morning's tea compliment.' And, while her heart played a merry tune within her, 'Hotch over,' he ordered, and as she moved over to make room he sat down on the side of the bed facing her. 'Sleep well?' he asked.

'Like a top,' she replied, having no idea what a top was, but having heard the expression somewhere, and very conscious of the virility of him, the smattering of hair on his chest showing through the neck of his short robe. 'Er—it looks like being a nice day,' she said hurriedly.

'Which reminds me—I have to be in London late this afternoon. I thought we'd have a leisurely morning and have lunch somewhere on the way back to your place?'

'Fine,' she agreed.

'I've a busy two weeks ahead of me and might be a bit pushed to see you. But if anything crops up, or you think of something you feel you may have a problem with, let my PA know. She'll know where to contact me—I'm on the move in foreign climes,' he explained.

'I think my mother's got most everything the way she wants it,' Lydie answered, already starting to feel desolate that he would be out of the country for the next two weeks.

'Apart from your bouquet,' Jonah teased.

'And the invitation list my mother wants closed but keeps thinking of other people we just *have* to invite. Your mother's doing the same, apparently.'

'So I believe,' he commented, revealing to Lydie that she wasn't the only one on the receiving end of motherly gripes. Though his expression had suddenly become stern when he said, 'My mother showed me the latest update to the invitation list your mother faxed her.' His tone had altered and Lydie knew something was wrong, even before he said, 'I wasn't going to bring it up—mainly because I couldn't believe my suspicions. But, since we're talking invitations, who's this Charles Hillier you've invited?'

Lydie stared at Jonah, her spirits taking a dive. 'You know quite well who he is,' she replied solemnly.

'I thought we agreed you were going to dump him?'

'He's my friend!' she protested. 'And I never agreed to "dump" him, as you call it. He's Donna's brother and—'

'And your one-time lover!' Jonah cut her off, somewhat aggressively she thought.

'He's not my lover!' she denied sharply, pulling the bed covers up over her shoulders defensively.

'He was!'

'He never was!' she retorted, outraged.

'You've slept with him!' Jonah replied, his eyes glittering a darker blue.

'Who told you that?' she demanded, feeling amazed. All this because she hadn't obeyed orders and 'dumped' a good friend?

'You did!' Jonah answered curtly, his chin jutting at an aggressive angle.

'When?' she challenged hostilely.

'You said, and I quote, "I stayed over with Charlie"—which meant you'd slept over at his place with him.'

Lydie felt a touch awkward as she recalled how she had known at the time that Jonah had thought

Charlie was her boyfriend but from some peculiar sense of pride she had declined to put him straight on that issue.

'If you remember that then you'll also remember I told you people are always misinterpreting me!'

Jonah studied her, his expression unsmiling. 'You're saying now that you did *not* spend the night at his place?'

'I'm not saying that at all!' she denied. 'I've stayed over at Charlie Hillier's place several times when I've been in London and it's been late or more convenient to stay over with Charlie in preference to driving to wherever...' She shrugged. Love Jonah though she did, she did not want this conversation. 'I know you said we should talk of all sorts without embarrassment,' she told him coldly, 'but I'm not happy with this conversation.'

His look said Tough and his voice was terse when, clearly not a man who enjoyed being messed about, 'Tell me straight, Lydie Pearson,' he demanded, 'have you ever had sex with this man?'

She resented his question. The day had seemed to start off so wonderfully—how had it become so ghastly? 'It's none of your business who I had sex with or did not have sex with before you and

I became engaged!' she told him haughtily. 'And I'd be glad if you'd get out of my room!'

'I'll get out when I'm ready,' he gritted icily. 'And I'm making it my business!'

'On what basis?' she challenged angrily. Love him she might, but *honestly*!

'On the basis that there'll be no one in that church a week next Saturday with whom I've slept. I should have thought common courtesy would decree you'd do me the same honour.'

Any further argument she might have found collapsed without trace. It was a pride thing! He was doing her the courtesy of not putting her in the position of having to shake hands with any of his bed-friends; pride demanded that he did not have to shake hands with any of her lovers.

Oh, Jonah! 'I had—when I stayed at Charlie's place—I had my own room,' she admitted at last. 'Charlie and I were never lovers. I slept alone. He is what I told you he is—a friend.'

Some of the aggressiveness left Jonah's expression, but he still did not seem totally convinced. 'You're a very beautiful woman, Lydie,' he commented, and, as if it was the only conclusion that would fit, 'Does this Charlie, your friend, have some kind of a sexual hang-up?' Lydie was about to tell Jonah of Charlie's extreme shyness, but as if remembering her reaction, her consternation of yesterday when she had touched his naked chest, fingered his nipples, plus his surmise that she had not had many lovers, all at once Jonah was staring at her as if with new eyes. 'Or, Lydie, is it you?' he asked.

'W-what?'

'Do you have something against sex?' he pressed.

In view of the fact that they were to be married in under two weeks' time, Lydie supposed it was a fair question. That still did not make her feel any more comfortable with the subject, though.

She dropped her eyes down to the coverlet. 'I w-wouldn't know,' she replied huskily.

There was a pause and, when she would not raise her eyes, movement. And the next Lydie knew, Jonah had moved close and had taken a hold of her hands in his. 'You wouldn't know?' he questioned quietly. And, when she couldn't find her tongue, 'I know you're embarrassed with this subject,' he went on, 'and that traces of the paralysing shyness you've fought so valiantly to overcome still occasionally trip you up, but I honestly think this is a subject we should air.'

'I know you're right,' she whispered. 'And, and I've wanted to tell you because, because I felt you should know—' She broke off. Even her ears felt a fiery red.

'Know what?' Jonah asked, any aggressiveness gone completely, only understanding there in his eyes when, placing a hand beneath her chin, he raised her head and made her look at him. 'What is it you felt I should know?'

'Oh, Jonah,' she wailed, 'I feel such a fool.'

'Share it with me,' he coaxed gently.

And at his tone, knowing if she went any redder she would burst into flames, Lydie found the courage to tell him. 'I've no idea if I've a sexual hang up or not, because I've—er—I've—um—never tried—um—sex.'

Jonah's reaction was to at first look totally taken aback, and then, still appearing shaken, a warm melting look came into his eyes. 'Oh, sweet Lydie,' he murmured. 'Are you saying you have never—ever—made love with anyone?'

'D-does that make me a freak?'

He smiled. 'It makes you a joy,' he answered, and just sat looking at her for ageless moments until, a wealth of good humour there, 'Given that this is still a non-committed weekend, how do you feel about a little experimenting?' he queried.

'Oh, J-Jonah,' she stammered nervously.

'There's nothing to worry about—I won't let it go too far,' he assured her. And, that smile playing around the corners of his mouth, 'Did we have our morning kiss?' he asked.

Lydie swallowed. 'You've forgotten already?' she attempted, and heard his light laugh. Then, unhurriedly, Jonah was reaching for her.

It was a gentle kiss, at first. She felt his warm touch as he gathered her to him and their lips met. And, more because she wanted to meet him all of halfway in this experiment, Lydie placed her arms around him.

Jonah raised his head to look deeply into her green eyes but, seeing no fear there, only shyness to be nightdress-clad and in his arms, he tenderly laid his mouth over hers again.

Lydie felt his hands warm at her back as they stroked in gentle rhythm. Then his kiss was starting to deepen. It was a heady kiss, and for a moment Lydie was terribly unsure and held back. But because she adored him, and was starting to love these moments of close intimacy, when his arms firmed about her and he held her closer so she moved that little way forward, and held him close.

Excitement started to spiral upwards in her, mingling with love and tenderness for him. He traced delicate kisses down the side of her face, then to her throat, and she clutched at him when he trailed more kisses down to her shoulder.

When he moved the strap of her nightdress down, kissing over her shoulder and down to the swell of her breast, and she felt his lips on that part of her breast that was uncovered, so love for him tangled with modesty and shyness, and she pushed at him slightly.

Immediately Jonah raised his head, drawing back a little, his eyes on her eyes. 'You're still not ready for my kisses, Lydie?' he asked, reminding her of the way, when she had agreed to marry him, she had said she didn't think she was ready for his kisses just yet.

'It isn't that,' she replied honestly. 'I'm just—well—feeling a bit—all at sea. Perhaps I should go and put some clothes on.'

His answer was to smile a teasing kind of smile, 'Oh, Lydie, Lydie,' he murmured softly. 'I don't—hmm—think you're quite getting the hang of this.'

Naturally, as the implication of that remark hit her, Lydie felt pink again. Jonah was meaning that in this instance she should be thinking more in terms of taking clothes off than in putting clothes on.

She took a shaky breath and, looking at him, felt her heart swell with love for him. 'Teach me,' she whispered, and for long, long, rapturous minutes knew utter bliss when tenderly Jonah drew her to him and, after first burying his face in her tousled dark hair, showered her with gentle, exquisite, kisses until she felt she would literally swoon away.

She had never known such a heady feeling like it. And when Jonah drew back to look into her eyes she wanted more, yet more. 'I'm not scaring you, Lydie?' he asked softly.

'I'll let you know when,' she murmured dizzily, and he laughed lightly, and drew her close to him again.

Kiss after gentle, tender kiss they shared, and Lydie's heart was pounding so loud she thought he might hear it. Then gradually a new dimension was entering Jonah's kisses and so, too, was a fire of wanting starting to flicker into life within Lydie.

She pulled back, feeling a little shaken. Instantly Jonah relaxed his grip. 'I *am* scaring you?' he questioned, his eyes studying and serious.

She shook her head. 'I don't think I've any hang up,' she told him honestly.

'Sweetheart,' he breathed, and held her close again, his mouth over hers, sending thrilling darts shooting through her when the tip of his tongue found its way through her parted lips.

She gave a startled movement, but, afraid he would stop, apologised immediately. 'I'm sorry,' she whispered quickly.

'I'm going too fast for you.' He blamed himself.

For answer she placed her lips over his and tasted his mouth with her tongue. She heard his groan of pleasure, and was thrilled anew. It seemed right to tell him that she loved him, but shyness held her back.

Then Jonah was creating all manner of new sensations in her when one caressing hand moved from her back to take slow caressing hold of her firm swollen breast. She jerked back, but he understood that too. 'It's all right,' he soothed.

But she was shy of his intimate touch, and leaned into him, and he took his hand from her breast and held her quietly to him for long moments. 'Have we proved that I don't have any kind of hang-up?' she asked.

'Do you want me?' he asked, and helped her out by adding, 'In case you haven't realised it, I confess, my dear, that I want you.'

Again she so nearly told him that she loved him, but bit it back—her love was something he had just not asked for. 'I feel I'm stumbling about in the dark,' she confessed.

'Shall we stop?'

'I didn't say I wasn't enjoying it,' she replied, and he laughed a joyous kind of laugh.

'What a delight you are,' he breathed.

It wasn't a declaration of love, but to hear him say she was a delight was music to her ears. 'I want to touch you,' she admitted shyly. But was nervous when, without more ado, he removed his robe, tossing it to one side. She swallowed hard, her eyes glued to his chest, her peripheral vision taking in long naked legs and some kind of undergarment.

'I want to touch you too,' he said softly, and moments later his mouth was over hers while his hands moved to capture both her breasts. And, while her desire for him made her feel breathless, he tenderly moulded her breasts, his fingers moving to tease the hardened tips, while Lydie gripped his naked shoulders tightly. Then all at once he was calling a halt. 'Oh, Lydie, Lydie,' he said hoarsely, his fingers reluctantly pulling away from her breasts. She felt his firm grip as he took hold of her upper arms, and was on fire for him when, as though struggling to find an even tone, Jonah said, 'If we don't stop now, we're going to be in deep trouble.'

But he had awakened feelings in her that had been dormant, and, 'I don't want you to stop!' she cried. That was before modesty belatedly galloped in. 'I shouldn't say things like that, should I?' she asked, a little self-consciously.

'Oh, my dear,' he murmured. 'If we don't stop, I'm going to have to see you without this tantalising piece of equipment,' he said, touching the material of her nightdress.

'Oh!' she gasped, and knew she was not as immodest as she had a moment ago thought. The idea of sitting there without a stitch on was something she was not quite ready for.

'And worse,' he went on, trying to inject a little humour into what was a very heat-filled time of sharing, 'there's a great risk you might catch a glimpse of me without mine.'

Lydie went hot all over. 'Truly a fate worse than death,' she attempted.

'Oh, sweetheart!' he groaned, and they kissed again, and clung to each other until abruptly Jonah broke from her and turned and reached for his robe. Only when it was safely about him did he turn to look at her. 'All right with you if I go now?'

'The alternative?' she asked.

'You don't need to ask,' Jonah told her, his wonderful blue eyes looking warmly into hers. 'But, since I can safely say we've become more committed this weekend than I intended in our non-committed pre-marriage time together, I think perhaps I should go.'

He went then, but when, later, both of them showered and dressed, they met in the kitchen, there was no awkwardness at the heady moments they had shared together.

Though, while Lydie was feeling slightly amazed that he could so matter-of-factly make coffee, toast and conversation as though nothing untoward had taken place between them, she discovered a short while later that he was not feeling so matter-of-fact as she believed.

'Let's go out,' he suggested.

'I thought you wanted a leisurely morning,' she reminded him.

He paused, and, eyeing her wryly, he replied, 'I did, but that was before your response in our lovemaking threatened to push me over the edge.'

Lydie stared at him, her heart soon thundering again. 'Are you saying what I think you're saying?' she asked. And, confused to know if he was meaning that if they stayed confined to the house he might make more love with her, 'I wish I knew more about this lovemaking business,' she mumbled.

Jonah looked solemnly at her. 'All in good time, Lydie,' he promised. 'All in good time.' And she went pink, which seemed to delight him, and they went out for a drive for him to acquaint her more with the area and to collect the Sunday papers.

Perhaps because she knew that there was every chance that when they said goodbye she would not see him again until she stood beside him in church, Lydie found she had no appetite for lunch. Jonah did not appear to eat a great deal either, she observed, but she rather thought that was because his mind was more on the business he had to return to London for than the fact that he would not see her again for almost two whole weeks.

He came into the house with her when they reached Beamhurst Court and said hello to her parents. And, while her mother went into raptures to her about just the 'right' hat she had bought on Saturday, Lydie saw that Jonah and her father had wandered over to the other side of the room and seemed to be having a very satisfactory conversation. She saw them shake hands—and her heart sank—Jonah must be planning to leave at any moment.

They ambled back to her and her mother, and although Lydie hadn't a clue what they had been talking about, she saw they seemed the best of friends. Which meant all in all everyone was getting on famously. But Jonah was on the point of leaving, and she didn't want him to go. She might not see him again for two long weeks, and already her heart was aching.

'Jonah has business he has to attend to,' she announced—rather starkly, it seemed to her.

'You won't stay to dinner?' Hilary Pearson invited, and Lydie felt cheered that her mother was at last showing Jonah the warmer side of her nature.

Jonah charmingly declined, said goodbye to her mother, shook hands with her father again, and, when Lydie was ready to run up to her room and stay there until she saw him again, 'Coming to see me out, Lydie?' he asked.

They left her parents in the drawing room, and as they walked out to his car all Lydie could think was, Don't go, don't go. To counter the feeling, the fear that those words might actually spill out, 'Have a good trip,' she smilingly bade him as they halted at his car.

Jonah turned and looked down into her wide green eyes. 'Remember what I said. Any problems, anything at all, ring Eileen Edwards and she'll get a message to me.'

'I'll remember,' Lydie replied, and, just to show that she wasn't the smallest bit bothered that she might not see him again until she married him, 'Don't do anything I wouldn't do.'

'Which is guaranteed to curtail my—er—life.' Lydie laughed. The missing word there was 'sexual', as in 'sexual life'. 'You're even more beautiful when your face lights up in laughter,' Jonah told her.

'For that you may kiss me goodbye,' she allowed loftily.

Jonah reached for her, held her in his arms and looked long into her eyes. 'Did you think I wasn't going to?' he asked, but as his head came down, he did not require an answer. Their lips met, and with her heart thundering that familiar beat Lydie had the hardest work in the world not to throw her arms around him. She wanted to beg him to take her with him—but theirs was not a love match, and he would think her soft in the head.

He said not a word when he let her go. Just looked at her for a long silent moment or two. Then he was getting into his car and driving away.

Lydie walked back into the house, tears in her eyes. She loved him so much—and there were a whole thirteen days to be got through until she saw him again.

Lydie hoped each day to see or hear from Jonah, but heard not a word for over a week. It was a busy week, and she was glad it was so because her time with Jonah at Yourk House was starting to feel like light years away. Had they really kissed and caressed the way they had? Was she doing the right thing in marrying him the way she was? What alternative did she have? She recalled her father, his face happy and smiling when talking to a relative over the phone. She did not, she knew then, have any alternative. Her father was back to being the man he had been—and did not seem to have a care in the world.

The next week slowly dragged into being, and, after Saturday, her wedding day coming ever nearer, it was on Tuesday that Lydie packed up some of her clothes ready to take to Yourk House. She packed another couple of cases with clothes she thought she might need on honeymoon. They were spending Saturday night at Yourk House prior to jetting off to their honeymoon island on Sunday.

On Wednesday, with four days to go before her wedding, Lydie started to get nervous and began to experience grave doubts. When she received a phone call from Jonah, Lydie felt she would have been quite happy if he had called to cancel the whole thing.

'Where are you?' she asked tautly.

'Sweden.'

'When are you coming back?'

'You sound uptight, Lydie?'

'I'm sorry. I know ours isn't the normal head over heels thing—' well, not on his side anyhow '—but I think I'm just about in the worst stages of bridal nerves. We'll be all right, won't we, Jonah?' she asked him anxiously.

'Oh, my word, you are suffering.'

'I wish you were here,' she replied, totally without thinking. And, as she died a thousand deaths to have said such a thing, she quickly added, 'I've loads and loads of luggage to take over to Yourk House. You know,' she hurried on, 'my on-holiday clothes, and—um—stuff I'll need when I get back.'

'I should have thought of that,' Jonah replied. 'Mrs Allen will be there tomorrow if you've time to go over. I'll give her a call and tell her to give you a spare key—she always keeps several spares.'

'I—um...' Grief, she was feeling tongue-tied with the man—and she was marrying him in three days' time!

'We'll be all right, Lydie, I promise you,' Jonah came in to reassure her when she got stuck for words.

She felt wretched. 'I'll—um—see you on Saturday, then,' she said, and there seemed little else to say. She said a quick, 'Goodbye,' and put down the phone. Oh, heavens! She was going to be his wife in three days' time—she only hoped her nerves held out until then.

CHAPTER EIGHT

BY SATURDAY, while still in a state of nerves, Lydie knew that above all else she wanted to marry Jonah. She had no idea how they would fare together, but she would do her best to make her marriage to him work.

She was awake early; her mother was already up and doing. To Lydie's tremendous surprise, when if it had dawned on her at all that she would have breakfast in bed, she'd have thought their housekeeper would be delegated to bring it to her, Hilary Pearson herself came in carrying a breakfast tray.

Coping with her surprise, Lydie began, 'You shouldn't...'

'Yes, I should,' her mother contradicted. 'This is your special day, and my mother brought me my breakfast in bed on the day I married your father.'

'W—' Lydie broke off. 'Thank you,' she accepted gratefully.

'How do you feel?'

'I'm not sure yet,' Lydie confessed, adding truthfully, 'But inclined to think I should pinch myself to check I'm awake and it's all real.'

'Which is perfectly natural.' Her mother smiled, and to Lydie's astonishment went on to say, 'I'm sorry if you've had reason to think from time to time that I've been in training for The Most Miserable Old Trout Of The Year, but this has been a most difficult time for your father and me.'

'It must have been truly awful at times,' Lydie sympathised.

'Our—difficulties—came close to wrecking our marriage,' her mother admitted, but smiled cheerfully when she went on, 'But, thanks to Jonah, we've come through.'

'You're referring to that cheque he gave me?'

'That was our darkest moment. I'm extremely grateful to him, Lydie.' She smiled again. 'Even if I haven't always managed to show it. He has no idea of the headaches he caused when he gave me just six weeks to get everything ready for to-day.'

'You've worked very hard,' Lydie stated. 'And I do thank you.'

'I don't need your thanks; it's what I'm here for.' Hilary Pearson beamed. 'Though I will say some of it has been a nightmare. Now, eat your

breakfast and don't hurry to come downstairs—
the house is packed with your cousins and aunts.
Make the most of your peace and quiet,' she advised.

Her mother left her to go and check out the
breakfast room, ready to organise anyone who, in
her opinion, needed organising. She really had
worked hard, Lydie reflected, and knew that,
while perhaps her mother's sometimes acid
tongue might occasionally grate on her, she loved
her mother and her hard-working mother loved
her.

With nothing but the best good enough, Lydie
had protested fiercely about the cost of her wedding. Where was the money coming from? she
had wanted to know. The last time she'd made
her objections felt she had been told she was being a perfect pain and sharply requested not to
interfere again. From then on Lydie had tried not
to wince at the next 'must have' her mother had
thought of.

Her marriage to Jonah was taking place at two
that afternoon, and, while Lydie tried to keep to
her room, she might just as well had joined all
her relatives downstairs, for she had a constant
stream of visitors.

Donna, the only attendant who had not stayed
overnight, arrived at noon. Nick and their children

were with her, but Donna was the only one of them her mother allowed upstairs.

'Your dress is gorgeous, absolutely gorgeous!' Donna exclaimed, on seeing it hanging on the outside of the wardrobe. It was a dress of empire design, the bust embroidered with silks and pearls, with folds of the soft jersey silk material falling straight from beneath the bust to hem. It had short sleeves and a modest rounded neckline that would reveal just the merest hint of cleavage. With it Lydie would wear the pearls her parents had given her for her twenty-first birthday, and the whole ensemble would be completed with a full-length veil kept in place by the family diamond and pearl tiara borrowed from her father's sister. The tiara was passed down the female line and would one day be passed down to Lydie's cousin Emilia.

Lydie had bathed when she had got up, but at twelve-thirty she decided to shower prior to getting ready. If it was supposed to be a tranquil time for her—it was not. Apart from the fact that one or other of her cousins had arrived yesterday without some essential to complete their toilet, and charged in to borrow a brush, a comb, a hair-dryer, Lydie had started to be swamped by her nerves.

She couldn't wait to see Jonah, but heartily wished this day were over. Nerves were well and truly getting to her. She had long since overcome that dreadful shyness of adolescence but, with all these people about, it seemed to have returned with a vengeance. She wished she had never agreed to a large wedding—though, recalling the way her mother had gone into action, did not think she'd had very much choice. Lydie was glad when everyone went to get dressed.

She seated herself before her dressing table mirror. Solemn green eyes stared back at her. In a little over an hour she would become Mrs Jonah Marriott—she felt all trembly inside at the thought.

At one-fifteen her four attendants came to her room. 'How do we look?' the beautiful Kitty asked, giving a little twirl in her empire line dress of midnight-blue.

'Beautiful,' Lydie answered. 'You all do.'

'Now you, Lydie,' said Donna, and as chief attendant and matron of honour she firmly pushed the others out. Lydie, her night-dark hair looped into a crown on the top of her head, and with the small amount of make-up she wore in place, was ready to slip on her dress. All that remained was to place her veil and tiara around the crown of her hair.

Donna seemed stuck for words when, having helped Lydie, she stood back to look at her. 'Will I do?' Lydie asked.

'Oh, Lydie, you look sensational!' Donna exclaimed, and looked quite weepy.

As did Hilary Pearson when she came into the room a minute later—the mail which had been forgotten about earlier forgotten again when, seeing her daughter in her bridal finery, she dropped the post down on Lydie's dressing table, and, 'Oh, darling,' she cried, 'what I picture you look!'

'So do you,' Lydie said lightly—that or have the whole three of them in tears. But her mother, in heels higher than normal for her and a wonderful frothy hat, did look superb.

Her mother stepped towards her, looking as though she might give her a hug, but, as if fearing to spoil or crease her dress, stepped back again. 'Right,' she said, adopting a bracing tone, 'it's time the bridesmaids were on their way to church,' and, ushering Donna out in front of her, she went to get them organised.

Lydie looked at herself in the full-length mirror when they had gone. Would Jonah think her a sensational picture? Remembering the stunning blonde, Freya, Lydie rather thought he was used to sensational.

But she did not want to dwell on thought of his past 'friends'; her stomach was churning enough without that. Lydie found a distraction in the mail her mother had brought in. There was an array of wedding cards, which she would open later, but there was also one letter. It was from a firm of solicitors.

Lydie checked that it was addressed to her and decided she had time to open it—and did. And almost collapsed in shock. The solicitors were executors for Alice Mary Gough, and Lydie, it appeared, was her aunt's sole beneficiary. By her will, Miss Gough had left her the house known as No. 2 Oak Tree Road, in the village of Penleigh Corbett. 'We have obtained the keys from the local authority, to whom they were inadvertently delivered, and shall be pleased if you will call and sign for them.'

Lydie read the letter through twice and, her eyes misting over, she had just slid the letter back into its envelope and placed it back on her dressing table when her parents came into her room.

Her parents spoke both together. Her father to say, 'Oh, my baby girl, how lovely you are!'

Her mother said, 'I'm going now,' and, catching sight of her daughter's misty eyes, 'Oh, please don't cry, Lydie, you'll start me off.' She then swallowed noisily and turned abruptly to her husband. 'I shall expect you to leave in exactly twelve minutes' time, Wilmot.'

'Yes, dear,' he answered sweetly.

'And don't laugh at me!' she commanded.

'No, dear,' he said, and, relieving the tension, they all three laughed.

Left alone with her father, though, Lydie just had to question, 'I thought Aunt Alice rented her house from the council?'

The perfect father, he didn't turn a hair, but took her question as the sort of question brides normally ask when they are trying to concentrate on something else to take their mind off the nerves they are enduring. 'She did,' he replied. 'For years and years. In fact she'd been a tenant for so long, paid rent for so long, that when— under some government scheme—she had the chance to buy it from the council she could have bought it for some ridiculously low price. She never had any money, as you know, but I did offer to lend her all she needed. She wouldn't take it, of course.'

'You didn't lend her the money?'

'It was only a trifling sum, but she was too proud to take it. Said, quite snootily, that she didn't care to be beholden to your mother. She was a stubborn old bat—lost a property that must be worth something in the region of a hundred and fifty thousand at today's prices.' He glanced at his watch. 'We'll have to go in a few minutes. Now, don't worry,' he went on cheerfully, 'I wouldn't let you go to Jonah if I wasn't fully convinced he'll do right by you.'

They went down the staircase with Lydie starting to realise that her great-aunt must have managed to scrape together the money to buy her house—and, typically Great-Aunt Alice, had kept her business to herself. Lydie did not want her house, she would much rather that her great-aunt would be in church to see her married that day.

Mrs Ross, who was keeping a sharp eye on the caterers, came to see her before she left her home for the last time as a single woman. But the housekeeper's eyes filled with tears when she saw her, and all she was able to say, before she handed Lydie her bouquet from the hall table, was a choked, 'I know you'll be very happy.'

Lydie thanked her. The bouquet of pink and white lisianthus was gorgeous, and worth the battle. She left her home to the sound of church bells, but on the short ride to the church Lydie, beset by nerves, could only think of Jonah waiting for her. She would make him a good wife, she *would*, she vowed—and then, out of nowhere, she was assaulted by the most torturous realisation that— she should not be marrying him!

And it wasn't just nerves. Her reason for marrying him, apart from her deep love for him that he knew nothing about, was because he had given her a cheque for fifty-five thousand pounds that she could not pay back. For her father, who had been hurting like the blazes that there was no way he could pay an outsider that money, she was marrying Jonah in order that he should be an insider.

Thoughts were rioting around in her head at a tangent. Jonah hated to be cheated. He was marrying her—yes, because he had decided it was time for him to marry—but, on thinking about it then, in her het-up state, she was sure a lot of that decision stemmed from having witnessed for himself the near broken man her father had been! A man then nothing like the buoyant man her father was today. Jonah had the highest respect for her father—but would Jonah have any respect for her when he knew that, thanks to her legacy from her great-aunt, he need not marry at all? His intended bride could pay him back. She could sell the property and return that fifty-five thousand pounds to him. Lydie gasped in shock as the realisation hit her that to marry Jonah would be—*to cheat him*!

'You're very pale,' her father said in concern as they arrived at the church. 'Are you all right, Lydie?'

She should tell him. Tell him that the wedding was off. 'Fine,' she murmured faintly, her head in turmoil as they walked up the path to where her attendants were waiting in the sunshine.

All before she had been able to marshal any coherent thought, her bridesmaids were falling in behind her. And while Lydie, nerves grabbing her by the throat, was reeling from her thoughts, in the next instant so the organist changed from the Handel he had been playing to Wagner's 'Bridal March' from 'Lohengrin' and the congregation rose to its feet.

I'll talk to the vicar. Lydie's thoughts raced in panic. I'll whisper to him that I need to speak to my fiancé in private. I'll... She saw Jonah up ahead, tall and straight in his morning suit, and suddenly she couldn't think of anything but that she loved him so heartbreakingly much and wanted so to marry him, to be his wife.

Swiftly she looked from him to her left, where her mother, her brother and his new wife were standing. Her mother would kill her if she cancelled now. After all her labours, her hair-tearing, her mother would probably never speak to her again if now, at the very last minute, with everyone there to witness it, she called the wedding off.

Lydie looked to the front again, and she and her father arrived next to Jonah and his best man, his brother Rupert. Lydie's thoughts were in total disarray when she felt that Jonah was looking at her. She turned her head to look at him—he smiled at her—and quite simply she loved him so much that what she should do and what she did were poles apart. She married him.

It was as if in a dream that Donna relieved her of her bouquet, that her father gave her away, and all Lydie was conscious of was of Jonah. Her voice was husky; his voice was firm, unhesitating as they exchanged their vows. Their eyes met, and she felt like melting at the warm encouragement in his superb blue eyes—as if he was very aware of the dreadful shyness that had chosen that day of all days to roar in and trounce her.

His touch on her shaking hand was magical, tender, as he placed his ring on her marriage finger—and they were declared man and wife. Shortly afterwards, the marriage register signed, witnessed, and all formalities completed, the organist was breaking out into 'The Wedding March' from Mendelssohn's *A Midsummer Night's Dream*. And, with her hand through Jonah's arm, they were soon heading the procession back up the aisle and going out into the sunlight, the bell ringers again busy.

They stood together at the church steps, people milling around, photographers, professional and amateur beavering away. Jonah bent to her. 'I know you've heard all the compliments, but out of this world doesn't begin to cover how indescribably lovely you look, Lydie.'

'Thank you,' she murmured. But by then her brain had started to wake up, and the enormity of what she had just done began to thunder in. *She had cheated him!* Oh, my... She should tell him. She saw her mother—beaming.

'You're still shaking,' Jonah bent to say quietly. 'We'll be...'

'Jonah, I...' There were people everywhere, friends, family, everyone smiling, everyone in first-class humour.

'Gone shy Lydie?' he teased, perhaps to help her feel a little less strung up when, having interrupted him, she had nothing more to add. She couldn't answer. He'd hate her when she told him. And tell him she would have to.

Though in the following hours, although they were together the whole time, there was not the smallest chance of any kind of a private conversation. And Lydie's nerves stretched and frayed.

She had stood with him to greet the guests. Had introduced people to him he had not previously met; he had done likewise. Charlie Hillier came and kissed her cheek and she introduced him to her new husband. Jonah weighed Charlie up in two seconds' flat, and was charming to him. Then Jonah was introducing someone called Catherine—and as Lydie shook hands with her she could not be jealous because she trusted Jonah not to allow her to shake hands on this day with any of his old flames.

And all the while that was what was getting to her—she could trust Jonah but, by cheating him, he could not trust her!

They sat down to a meal that was quite splendid; her mother would not have countenanced anything else. Then the speeches began. First Rupert made a humorous speech—Catherine, seated next to him, turned out to be his latest in a long line of girlfriends. Then Lydie's father made a wonderful speech where he let everyone know that if he'd had to personally choose a husband for his dear daughter he would not have done better than to have made the choice she had made. Then Jonah was on his feet, his speech short but sounding sincere when he said that he would want for nothing more than to be married to Lydie.

Had that been true Lydie felt she would have fainted away on the spot from the sheer joy of it. But as spontaneous applause broke out, and her mother and Jonah's mother, and even Kitty, seemed quite moist-eyed, Lydie knew that it was not true.

In fact she started to think that all of it was a sham, and she was heartily glad when the time came that she could disappear up to her room to change. She needed to be by herself. Though in actual fact she had time only to read through again the letter from her great-aunt's solicitors and to slip it inside her handbag—oh, why had it had to arrive today?—before her cousins and Donna were in her room to help her change. Lydie was quite able to change without assistance, and could have done without company just then, but tradition was tradition, she supposed.

'Are you feeling all right, Lydie?' Donna asked under cover of the three cousins hooting with laughter at some tale of Gaynor's. 'You seem quiet, if you know what I mean.'

'I'm absolutely fine,' Lydie answered. 'It's been a bit of a long day, though, hasn't it?'

'You should be home by eight, nine o'clock at the latest. And you'll have two whole months on your island in which to recuperate.' Donna smiled.

From where Lydie was viewing it, she would be very surprised if, after she had told Jonah what

she had to tell him, they would be going anywhere. Forget the honeymoon.

Though, with their goodbyes seeming to take
for ever, Lydie started to think they would be
lucky if they reached Yourk House by nine that
evening, let alone eight. And by the time she was
at last alone with Jonah, she was feeling so uptight she didn't think she would be able to say a
word to him. Yet she must. Before this day was
out he had to be told—that his wife was a cheat!

'Alone at last!' Jonah commented as he swung
his long sleek car out past the gates of Beamhurst
Court.

Tell him! Lydie opened her mouth—and closed
it again. 'Jonah…' she tried, but her voice
sounded all kind of cracked and strangled in her
ears and she could find nothing to add.

Jonah glanced at her and smiled, one hand
leaving the steering wheel briefly to take her hand
in a reassuring squeeze. 'Try to relax, Lydie,' he
said kindly. And, his smile deepening, 'You know
I don't bite.'

Oh, heavens, he thought she was nervous with
him. That on this, her bridal night, she was tense
and starting to get worried. But it wasn't that—
she longed to be in his arms, ached for his kisses.
She had not seen him for almost two long weeks.
Almost two long weeks since she had last been

in his arms, had last been held by him, held and…
She blanked her thoughts off and closed her eyes,
and was tormented all the way to Yourk House.
She wanted to be his wife. But that word 'cheat'
rattled around and around in her head. Cheating.
Was that any way to start to build a marriage?

'Tired?' Jonah asked as they pulled up at
Yourk House.

Lydie guessed he could be forgiven for thinking that. Her replies to any conversation he had
attempted had been monosyllabic to say the least.
She found refuge in the answer she had given
Donna earlier.

'It's been a—a bit of a long day,' she replied,
and as Jonah got out of the car and came round
to the passenger side she quickly stepped out—in
consequence bumping into him.

She would have turned away, but the hands that
came out to steady her continued to hold on to
her. Lydie looked up into a pair of fantastic, understanding blue eyes.

'Stop worrying. I'm not a monster.' He gave
her a small shake. 'We don't have to seal our
marriage tonight. We've got two whole months
in which to intimately get to know each other.'
He smiled encouragingly. 'There's no rush.'

She stared at him, all thoughts of how she had cheated him gone temporarily from her mind. 'You—don't want to make love to me?'

He laughed. It was wonderful to see. 'Oh, Lydie,' he said softly, 'have you got a lot to learn.' And, so that she did not misinterpret his reply, 'I want you, quite desperately, but I want more desperately that everything is right for you.'

Lydie looked at him, startled. But before she could begin to assess what, if anything, he meant by that last bit, he had picked her up in his arms and was carrying her over to the front door of Yourk House.

'Traditional, I believe,' he murmured, unlocked the door, and carried his bride over the threshold of her new home.

He did not set her down until they were in the drawing room. And by then Lydie's thoughts and emotions were all over the place. Her heart was racing just to be so close to him. Don't tell him, urged the part of her that wanted so badly to stay with him. Why tell him? If that letter from those solicitors hadn't come today she would have been married to him for two whole months before either of them knew anything about it. By then they would have grown to know each other intimately. Perhaps by then Jonah, her husband, would have begun to care for her a little. Who knew? Don't tell him.

He lowered her to the floor, and she stood with him in the circle of his loose hold. 'Mrs Ross will have left us some supper,' he began.

But Lydie was shaking her head. She was starting to get confused. Food would choke her. 'I'm—not hungry,' she said quickly, her voice sounding all kind of staccato even to her ears.

'You've had a busy day,' Jonah answered, 'chatting to all our guests with never a minute to yourself. Would you like to go to bed?' he asked. And, when she went to jerk out of his hold, 'Shh,' he quieted her, but kept her there in his arms. 'You're trembling,' he murmured, and smiled reassuringly as he tried to ease the new moments of being alone at the start of their married journey together. 'We'll share a bed, but until you feel comfortable having me there next to you we'll just lie together.'

'Oh, Jonah!' she cried, emotional tears welling up inside as she coped with a feeling of being stunned that he should be so considerate, so thoughtful. 'You're so kind.'

He looked at her, his mouth curving wryly. 'Does that entitle me to kiss my bride?' She stared at him, her heart going wild within her. And, when she was too choked to speak, Jonah appeared to take that as an indication that she had no objection. Because a moment later he was drawing her that little bit nearer and his head was coming down—and his lips were claiming hers.

It was a gentle kiss, a tender kiss, and when he pulled back they just stood staring into each other's eyes. What he was reading in hers she had no idea. Certainly there was no objection there to his kiss. And, as he drew her that little bit nearer still, Lydie did not have any objection to make when he kissed her again.

Of their own volition her arms went around him, and suddenly she was on the receiving end of a kiss that made her legs wilt. 'My wife,' he murmured against her mouth, and as she responded their bodies came close, and they kissed and moulded to each other.

She loved him so, and her lips parted voluntarily to allow the tip of his tongue to enter. She pressed to him and felt a fire scorch through her when he moved his hands to her hips and he pulled her yet closer to his wanting body.

And her body was wanting too. 'My wife', he had called her. She was his wife. Joy started to break in her. But as the words 'My wife' throbbed through her, and passion between them mounted, so that part of her that was essentially honest chose just that moment to rocket in and bombard her.

Wife! She had no right to be his wife. She felt his hands on her skin beneath the short jacket of her suit. Felt the bliss as he caressed her silken skin. He kissed her again, ardently, his hands caressing her back, her bra a barrier to that caressing. He unclasped her bra, his hands travelling freely, deliciously, over her soft smooth back while his tongue penetrated that little bit further. His mouth was still over hers, creating mayhem to her senses when his palms moved round to her ribcage. She felt his warmth and seemed not to be breathing at all when his loitering hands inched their way up under her bra. Then in breath-holding moments his hands caressed their way ever upwards until both her firm breasts were in his hold. Again he kissed her, and as his fingers made a nonsense of all coherent thought in her he stroked and moulded in exquisite torment around the hardened peaks of her breasts that welcomed and wanted more. Instinctively she pressed into him, hearing his small sound of wanting; it was how she felt too.

He kissed her again, and his mouth was still over hers when his reluctant fingers left her breast, and with that hand caressing the side of her face he looked deep into her eyes, and softly breathed, 'I think we'll be more comfortable up-stairs, don't you?' He bent, as if to pick her up in his arms and carry her to their marriage bed.

Her sharp, *'No!'* stopped him, though she hardly knew from where that protest had come. He was her husband and she wanted to be his wife.

Arrested by her protest, he stared at her, as well he might—she had been giving him very affir-mative signals. 'No?' he echoed.

'I—c-can't,' she stuttered, and knew that she could not. She loved him too much to cheat him. If she said nothing, she would be his wife—their marriage consummated. It was what she wanted. She wanted to be part of him, of so much, to share her body with him, to share his body. But—no! It could not be. It had to stop. With her heart aching she turned her back to him and did up her bra, and, her throbbing, wanting breasts once more confined, she straightened her jacket and turned to him. He was looking nowhere but at her, a thoughtful expression on his face.

'Okay,' he said calmly after a second or two, 'let's go back five minutes. I'll apologise for what's just happened if you want me to, but you're a very desirable woman, Lydie—you'll have to forgive that my antennae read it wrong.

So we'll go upstairs—but perhaps you'd better sleep alone tonight after all.'

'Oh, Jonah. It's not—' She broke off, shyness belatedly arriving so that she could not tell him that it was not that she did not want to follow where he lead in their lovemaking, but that it was not right that she should. 'I can't...' she said helplessly.

'You don't have to tonight. I've already said...'

'I can't—*ever*,' she butted in, because she had to.

'Ever?' He looked puzzled, and as if he was trying to work out what was going on here.

'Never,' she replied chokily.

'Oh, Lydie,' he sympathised. 'Your nerves are shot. Don't worry, after a night's rest, everything will—'

'Our marriage will have to be annulled!' she butted in quickly, while she could still find the strength.

'*Annulled?*' Oh, heavens, she could see that Jonah did not care at all for this development. Though his tone was controlled when he quietly asked, 'You don't think I might have a little something to contribute to that decision?'

'You don't understand,' Lydie said desperately, keeping her distance from him—she still felt all of a tremble from his kisses and needed all the strength she could find. Though she rather thought, knowing his strong aversion to being cheated, that he would help her on her way when she told him what she had to tell him.

'You're right there. I don't understand,' he replied.

'I—I cheated you,' Lydie confessed, her heart falling into her shoes when she saw him frown— he did not take kindly to hear he had been cheated, she could tell. She hurried on, 'I have the money—or will have. The fifty-five thousand! I knew it just before I left for the church,' she admitted breathlessly. And, as she had to, 'I should never have married you,' she owned shakily.

What she expected once that stark confession was out in the air, Lydie was not sure. Probably that, hating that anyone should attempt to cheat him, Jonah would send her back to Beamhurst Court without delay. That, she having cheated him, would be got rid of *tout de suite*. Their marriage annulled before the ink on their wedding certificate was set.

What she had not expected was that Jonah would be remotely interested in knowing more than that she had cheated him. But, to her consternation, he fixed her with a stern look and, 'You've just said you should never have married me,' he took up toughly. And, looking directly into her anxious green eyes, he as toughly added, 'Then perhaps, my dear, you'll have the courtesy to explain exactly why you did?'

Lydie stared at him, numbed. She wasn't ready for this. She need not have married him for her father's sake; she had known that before she had reached him at the altar. It therefore followed that she had married him solely because she loved him and had wanted to marry him more than she had wanted anything in her life. But there was no way she was going to tell him that. Though, with Jonah standing there watching, waiting, everything about him was telling her that she was going nowhere until she had given him an explanation—but what explanation could she possibly give?

CHAPTER NINE

LYDIE had still not answered him when Jonah, his expression telling her he was insistent on having that answer, sifted through what she had said and, to her great alarm, bluntly asked, 'Why marry me at all, Lydie, when you knew that you did not have to?'

'It was too l-late,' she stammered, and, clutching at straws, 'My mother would have murdered me had I called everything off at the last moment.'

'You've stood up to your mother before when you felt strongly enough about something,' he reminded her, and dissected in an instant what she had said. His face darkening, he came back to challenge, 'You're saying you cheated me, but didn't feel strongly enough, guilty enough about it, to risk your mother's displeasure and not marry me?'

'It wasn't… I… Oh…' She was floundering and knew it. 'I d-didn't get, read, the letter from Aunt Alice's lawyers until a short while before I was due to leave the house for the church.'

'Your great-aunt left you some money?'

'She left me her house. I didn't even know Aunt Alice owned it, but she must have. Her lawyers…'

'So you married me, despite knowing that once that house is sold—I take it you aren't intending to live in it?' he inserted, sounding hostile, 'you'll have sufficient funds to be out of my debt?'

Lydie nodded. 'From what my father said—'

'You've discussed this with your father?' he cut in sceptically.

'No! Only to say I thought Aunt Alice rented her house. He doesn't know about the letter. He said that Aunt Alice had the chance to purchase her house very cheaply some years ago and that, had she done so, it would be worth about a hundred and fifty thousand pounds today.' Lydie swallowed on a dry throat, and went tremulously on. 'Once I've repaid my debt to you, there should be sufficient over to pay the caterers and any outstanding items from t-today.'

Jonah heard what she had to say and, his eyes on her, he seemed to silently deliberate. He took a pace away and half turned from her, his mind occupied. But then, as if he had reached a decision, he turned back to her, and, his eyes steady on hers, he quietly let fall, 'I think you'll find, Lydie, that all accounts—apart from yours and mine—have been settled.'

Wordlessly Lydie stared at him, questions rushing to her lips. All accounts—apart from theirs? What did that mean? She shelved that question, pride giving her a nasty time as she asked, appalled, 'You didn't pay for my wedding? You didn't ask for all bills to be sent to you?' And, feeling mortified with embarrassment, 'My father didn't allow you to finance today's—'

'Would he?' Jonah interrupted. And, not waiting to hear her reply, stated firmly, 'He would not.' Jonah paused, and after a moment quietly informed her, 'Trust me, your father can well afford to settle for today's function without it hurting too much.'

Lydie didn't believe it. 'The last I heard was that he was broke. My mother called me a pain because I've worried so much about today's expense.' And, feeling hostile herself, even though she knew that she was the one in the wrong here, 'Now you're telling me I need not have worried at all? I don't believe it!' she snapped.

'Why should you believe it?' Jonah agreed. But, his hostility fading suddenly, 'Come and sit down,' he suggested, indicating one of the sofas, 'and I'll explain...'

'There's nothing for you to explain.' Lydie cut him off agitatedly. She had an idea that he might decide to share that sofa with her—and she had been closer to him than was good for her not so long ago. 'I cheated you. You'll want an annulment, and that's all there is to it.'

Jonah looked at her for long, long moments, then, with his glance fixed on hers, his tone perfectly audible, 'Correction, Lydie,' he clearly said, '*I* cheated you. I married you because I wanted to. And there is *no way* this marriage is going to be annulled.'

Her insides started to churn more fiercely. She knew he had wanted to marry, that he had decided it was time he married. But her? 'You could have married just about anybody, it didn't necessarily have to be me.' She spoke her thoughts out loud. And what had he just said about him cheating her? It was she who had cheated him! 'I must be more tired than I thought. None of this is making sense.'

'Would you like to go to bed? We can have this discussion when we get to the island tomorrow.'

'You still want to go on our honeymoon?' she asked, her eyes widening in surprise.

'Have you forgotten so soon? I told you when I asked for your promise to marry me that divorce is not an option. The same goes for an annulment.'

Suddenly her legs felt as if they were about to give way. To sit down seemed a good idea. By the sound of it, even though she had confessed to having cheated him, Jonah still wanted to stay married to her.

'I think I'll…' she mumbled, and went over to the sofa. Jonah surprised her by taking a chair close by—opposite her. Realising that she had no chance of hiding her expression from him, Lydie lowered her gaze as she apologised. 'I'm sorry I married you when as soon as Aunt Alice's house is sold I shall be able to repay that loan.'

'And I'm sorry you feel you have to repay it,' Jonah answered. 'But, if it will make you feel better, I have to tell you that the fifty-five thousand was repaid, with the accumulated interest your father insisted upon, a couple of weeks ago.'

Her head shot up. 'Repaid!' Her brain wasn't taking this in. 'Who repaid it?' she asked. And, as her intelligence started to go into action, 'Are you saying that—I needn't have married you?' She wasn't sure she did not go pale; she felt pale. 'You said…' She struggled to recall what exactly he had said. 'You said y-you had cheated me. Is that what you meant? That you had cheated *me* into marrying *you*?' That couldn't be. She had cheated him! 'Would you explain? I didn't think I'd drunk too much champagne, but I'm not coping with this at all well. Who repaid you that money? My father doesn't have any, and...' She stopped, feeling totally perplexed.

That feeling wasn't helped much when all at once Jonah left his seat and came over and took a seat on the sofa next to her. 'Poor love,' he murmured, and, catching a hold of her hands in his, 'This moment has come far sooner than I'd anticipated,' he continued. 'But perhaps it's as well that we start our marriage with certain matters out of the way.'

'You're still insisting that we stay married?' she asked, a touch shakily.

'It's the only way,' he replied, which told her precisely nothing.

'I can pay you—or will be able to pay...'

'Your father has already done so.'

'My father doesn't have any money!'

'He does now.'

'How?' Lydie questioned. 'Only a couple of months ago he was in deep despair that he'd sold everything he could possibly sell. Where did he get the money?'

Jonah was half turned to her. Lydie, pulling her hands from his hold, half turned to look at him, her eyes pleading for answers. 'Your father,' Jonah began, 'has sold a half of Beamhurst Court.'

Shocked to hear such a thing, Lydie stared at him in utter astonishment. 'He wouldn't!' she exclaimed. 'My mother wouldn't allow him!'

'She did,' Jonah stated calmly.

And Lydie just sat stunned. Jonah sounded as though he knew it for the truth. Half a dozen questions jostled for precedence in her head. Her father had sold half of Beamhurst Court? Unbelievable! Her mother had sanctioned it? Impossible! And how was Jonah so much in the know, Lydie wondered, when she, the daughter of the house, had been totally in the dark about it? And… Abruptly then, though, a whole new question burst in on her intelligence.

'You said that fifty-five thousand pounds was repaid to you a couple of weeks ago?'

'That's right,' Jonah agreed—but seemed to be already anticipating her next question.

He showed no surprise anyhow when, quite a bit startled, she had to admit, Lydie slowly questioned, 'Then, if that money was repaid, my father no longer in your debt—why did I marry you? You let me marry you,' she went on, feeling winded, 'when there was absolutely no need whatsoever for me to marry you.'

'I'm afraid there was. Apart from other considerations,' Jonah commented, 'you had told your father that I'd some proposition to put to him.'

'You told him you were going to ask me to marry you.' She reminded him of what he had said.

'That was part of it.'

'Part? But not all?'

Jonah shook his head. 'It had to be part, for the rest of it to follow,' he explained, but when Lydie looked totally mystified he revealed a little more detail. 'At the same time of telling me how you'd told your father I'd a proposition to put to him, you also told me how he had been prepared to sell Beamhurst Court. You mentioned too that your brother wasn't remotely interested in the property.'

By then her brain was working overtime. 'You found a buyer for my father? Someone interested in purchasing only a half of the property?' How on earth would that work? She couldn't see her mother sharing her home with anyone!

Lydie's puzzled eyes were fixed on nowhere but Jonah's wonderful blue eyes, when, quietly, he revealed, 'I am the buyer, Lydie.'

Her eyes went saucer-wide. 'You're the buyer?' she echoed faintly.

'While you and I will live here at Yourk House, as we planned, Beamhurst Court is now in the joint names of you and your father,' Jonah replied. And while she stared at him, thunderstruck by that astounding statement, 'I know how you love the place,' he added. 'I bought a half of it for you, Lydie.'

She stared at Jonah witlessly. 'You—bought it—for me?' Her voice was barely above a whisper. 'You…' It must have cost him a small fortune! 'You…' she tried again. 'My father…' It was no good. As what he had said started to sink in, she was so totally stunned she did not seem able to frame another sentence.

Looking at her, seeing how dumbstruck she was, Jonah took pity on her and began to elucidate. 'You'll remember, the day of your great-aunt's funeral, your father and I went to his study?'

'You said you'd gone to tell him that you wanted to marry me. You said that our being married would make you a family member, an insider, so my father wouldn't feel too badly about…' The small quirk on Jonah's superb mouth made her hesitate.

He smiled encouragingly, but corrected, 'Insider, nothing! Son-in-law or no, your father would never rest until he paid that money back. I *knew* that. He *knew* that. You, Lydie, thinking with your love for him and not your mind, were emotionally blinded by a sign that he might be returning to his old self, and *missed knowing* that.'

'But...' She broke off, a dawning realisation hitting her that it was just as Jonah had said—her father had started to brighten up and she hadn't looked further than to see him take a new lease on life, than to go along with whatever Jonah told her. 'Have I been incredibly naïve?' she asked, still feeling more than a mite shaken.

'No father could have a better daughter,' Jonah answered softly, and disclosed, 'Once I was in the study with him that day, I told him that I would very much like to marry his daughter. He at once gave me his blessing, and I then put the proposition you had suggested to him that I intended to.'

'But you didn't have a proposition.'

'Your father is well aware of your attachment to Beamhurst. I put it to him that I would very much like to have your name on the deeds as my wedding gift to you.'

'Oh, Jonah!' she whispered, unable to hold it back. But she grew suddenly terrified that he would see how his incredibly generous gesture had hit at the heart of her. From somewhere, she knew not where, she somehow managed to find some stiffening to her wilting backbone, and questioned, 'And my father, he agreed—just like that?'

'He said he would think about it, but I could see he was at once very taken with the idea. Anyhow, by the time you and I came back from our walk…'

'When you asked for my promise to marry you,' Lydie put in, her head starting to spin.

'Where you gave me your promise,' Jonah agreed. 'By that time your father had it all worked out. He suggested he and I return to his study to discuss my proposition in more in-depth detail.' Lydie remembered clearly. She had seen them heading for the study when she'd been on her way upstairs to change. 'Wilmot had by then seen the advantages: he would have money to settle what he considered his debt to me and have money at his disposal. Before we could get the property professionally valued and everything legally drawn up, though, he wanted me to understand that, should he sell, your brother would ultimately inherit his half. Also, he felt your mother would insist on an assurance, that should Oliver at some future date change his mind about wanting Beamhurst Court, you would sell your half to him. I agreed on your behalf on the assurance that, at some very much future date, we—you and

I—would have the first option to purchase, should Oliver wish to sell.'

She was spellbound that all this had gone one. 'And—my father consented?'

Jonah nodded. 'The deal was completed a fortnight ago—naturally in the utmost secrecy. I told your father I wanted to surprise you on our honeymoon with a copy of the deeds showing Lydie Marriott as joint owner.' Lydie Marriott. How wonderful that sounded. 'Wilmot felt he had to tell your mother, but he was certain, once she knew all details, that she would raise no objection and would, as was essential, keep our secret. So all in all,' Jonah ended, 'your father was again happy. Your mother, with money available to see you married in respectable fashion, was happy. And you, Lydie—' he smiled at her '—I'd like very much for you to be happy—but, I'm sorry, that does not include an annulment.'

Lydie knew that she wanted to stay married to him, but, while she did love Beamhurst, she just could not get over the fact that he had bought a half of it—for her!

'It's too much!' she exclaimed. 'You've solved all of our problems but—what about you? What do you get?'

'Oh, my dear,' Jonah answered softly. 'While it pleases me tremendously to see that look of strain gone from the face of a man I admire so much, what I have, this day, is you.'

Lydie stared at him. He was rather marvelous, this man she had married. And she knew that what he was actually saying was that, having decided to marry, he had this day got himself a wife. But—was that good enough?

'Is it—all right to marry when—love isn't there?' she asked, and, not wanting him to see how much it mattered to her, she looked away from him, her eyes giving her wedding band serious study in the lengthening tense kind of silence that followed.

Then she was at once wishing that she had never uttered a word about love. For as the tension, the silence stretched, she knew for certain that Jonah had never thought about love in any of this. She so desperately wished he would say something—the taut silence was getting to her.

Though when, after long moments of considering what she had said, Jonah did break the silence, he caused her to be totally panic stricken when he stated, quite clearly, 'But love is there.'

As soon as his words hit her ears Lydie was on her feet. She leapt from the sofa, her emotions in complete chaos. And had taken several rushed steps across the room before she was aware of it.

But, halting, turning to see that Jonah was on his feet too, she stared at him absolutely stupefied.

'You know I love you?' she gasped, horrified, and saw him freeze in his tracks—shaken rigid.

'What—did you say?' he clipped, his tone all kind of shocked, as if he could not believe his hearing.

'Nothing!' she denied, faster than the speed of light. 'I didn't say anything.'

But he wasn't having that, though still seemed too stunned to move. 'You said you love me,' he reminded her, when she needed not the smallest reminding. And, shaking his head as if dazed, 'I refuse to start off this marriage with lies, Lydie Marriott. Tell me the truth. Do you have feelings for me?'

She shook her head. Anybody would think it was important. 'It doesn't matter,' she answered, making a poor showing of the off-hand tone she had been hoping for.

'Of course it matters!' he retorted. A few yards separated them but neither of them was moving an inch, she as frozen now as him.

'W-why?' Oh, why had she said what she had? It was blatantly obvious now that Jonah had had no idea of her love for him.

'Why? Because...' He hesitated, paused, and, as if he had just come to a decision, his head came up a proud fraction as he said, 'I married you today, Lydie, purely because it was what I wanted to do.'

'For my father's sake,' she butted in. 'You married me because my father…'

'My decision to marry you had nothing at all to do with your father or anyone else.' Jonah set her straight. 'I married you for the reason I stated at our wedding reception, because—for weeks now—I've wanted nothing more than to be married to you.'

'Because you felt it was time for you to be married. That's what you said.'

'Oh, Lydie, Lydie, I have to tell you now that I discovered you are not the only one who can lie their head off,' he confessed, causing her to stare at him. But her eyes grew yet wider when he added, 'I am not lying now—nor will I ever lie to you again—when I tell you that I married you for no other reason than that I want, and need, to be with you for the rest of my life.'

Her breath caught in her throat. 'Y-you married me—for m-me?' she questioned with what breath she had left.

'I married you solely for you,' he confirmed. 'I married you, my dear, dear Lydie, because I one day woke up to the fact that I had fallen quite, quite hopelessly in love with you.'

Lydie stared at him in stunned amazement, a kind of roaring going on in her ears. 'You didn't!' she denied. And, remembering how sensitive he was with her sometimes, 'You're only saying that so I shan't feel I have made such a complete fool of myself.'

But already Jonah was shaking his head. 'No more lies, Lydie, from either of us.' She still didn't believe him. 'Come here,' he said. 'Meet me halfway. Let me hold you in my arms and convince you.' He took a step towards her; she took a panicking step back. He halted.

'Convince me from there!' she exclaimed. If he took her in his arms again she would be lost, would be deaf to anything but that which she wanted to hear.

Jonah smiled, as if he knew something of what she was going through. 'I'm feeling not a little emotionally shattered myself,' he admitted, every bit as if her statement that she loved him had knocked him sideways. 'Shall we at least sit down?'

It seemed the sensible thing to do, and just then Lydie felt very much in need of something sensible to latch on to. She went and sat in the chair he had occupied earlier.

She had expected he would use the sofa but he made her heart beats start to jump around again when he took hold of another chair and drew it up close, opposite hers.

They were almost touching knee to knee when Jonah, his eyes on her face, asked, 'Am I allowed to say how very beautiful you are, and how for me a day without you is a day without the sun?'

Oh, Jonah! If she hadn't been sitting down Lydie would not have given much for her chances of not collapsing into a chair. She strove to be sensible.

'This is you convincing me that you didn't say you l... what you said, purely from some kind of sensitivity because of w-what I said?'

'You said you loved me, Lydie,' he reminded her gently.

'Don't!' she moaned.

'Don't be embarrassed, my darling. While I'm still having the greatest trouble taking it in, in actually believing that it can possibly be true, I want you to believe that I love you so very much that at times it has been like a physical pain.'

Lydie stared at him, her green eyes huge. She knew that feeling. 'But—you never said. Never so much as hinted...'

'How could I? I was terrified of frightening you off.'

'You were terrified...' She found that hard to believe, and guessed her feeling of disbelief must have shown.

'I've sound reasons,' he cut in, 'which I suppose stemmed initially from having you as an extremely shy but charming sixteen-year-old imbedded somewhere in my mind.'

'I was still sixteen in your mind?' she queried, intrigued in spite of her shaky feelings inside.

'Only to start with. You were beautiful then. In the seven years since you have blossomed to be even more beautiful than my imaginings.'

'You'd thought of me—since then?'

'Off and on. I made a return trip to your home three years ago—to give your father the money I owed him. I'd hoped to see you, but you weren't around.'

'You wanted to see how I'd turned out?'

'Something like that, though I never actually put it into words. Anyhow, there I am, ten weeks ago, returning to the office from doing some negotiating overseas, to have my PA tell me that a Lydie Pearson was anxious to contact me.' He paused, and then owned, 'When at last I did see you, I found you quite captivating, my Lydie.'

Captivating? His? The whole of her felt weak. 'I wasn't very pleasant to you,' she commented, trying desperately hard to keep both feet on the ground.

'You thought I'd reneged on the debt I owed your father,' he reminded her gently. 'Somewhat to my own surprise, when it's usually my business head that rules me, I found I was reaching for my chequebook. As you know, I hold your father in high regard, and told myself I was writing that cheque because he had given me financial help when I asked for it. I knew full well that he was too honourable to ask for my financial help unless he could see a way of repaying it. But even while, as you rightly said, I was conning you into paying that cheque into the bank without delay, I was not thinking of being repaid—my head was full only of you.'

Lydie blinked. 'You mean, you—er—were attracted to me?'

'Oh, Lydie, I wasn't yet ready to admit some woman had started to tie me up in knots,' he answered, his lips quirking.

'I did that?'

'As I said, I wasn't admitting it. Though I have to say it came as a bit of a jolt to see you at the theatre with your friend Charlie. I didn't like it.'

Lydie searched the depths of his fantastic blue eyes. His gaze did not falter. Could he really love her? She was too stewed up by all that had happened and was happening to know. She decided to stick to fact, as she knew it. 'You said for me to come to your office the following Monday,' she remembered, but the way Jonah was looking at her, tenderly—dared she hope lovingly?—was making such a nonsense of her she could barely remember why she had gone to see him. 'I came to see you,' she struggled through, 'to discuss how I should repay that money.'

'And I found myself in a state of upheaval.'

'Upheaval?'

He smiled at her surprise. 'I wasn't bothered about the money. You were the one making an issue of it. But perhaps I could use that to my advantage.'

Lydie was stumped. 'Advantage?' She could not help repeating him again.

'I knew then that I wanted to see you again. Perhaps it was the last throes of my long-schooled wary bachelor faculty at work, perhaps it was because I knew that you were different—call it what you will—but, while I didn't want to deprive myself of your company, I decided that I didn't want any involvement. To see you at your brother's wedding seemed to me a good way to see you again while at the same time making our meeting less one-to-one personal.'

She was staggered. 'That's why you wanted that wedding invite!' She stared at him in amazement. 'But,' she began to recall, 'the very next day, after Oliver's wedding, when I came to see you at your apartment, you were suggesting that I come here to Yourk House and spend the weekend with you!'

'Why wouldn't I? You'd just told me you'd previously stayed overnight with your friend Charlie! I didn't care at all for the thought you might be spending the next Saturday night in some man's bed. I know, I know, you were never lovers, but I didn't know that then and, while I wasn't admitting to feeling a tinge green whenever I thought of you and him, dammit, I was as jealous as hell.'

Lydie was fairly reeling. Jonah, jealous of Charlie? 'You told me to dump him.'

But the next moment Jonah had taken her hands and was drawing her to her feet. 'Lydie, I can't take much more of this. I know I probably haven't convinced you yet, but I love you so much, and if you love me only half as much, you'll let me hold you.'

She stood with him. 'You want to hold me?'

'I need to hold you, my darling,' he murmured.

It only required one small step towards him. Lydie drew a shaky breath—then took that small step. And the next she knew, she was in his arms, held up against him in a gentle tender hold.

Jonah held her like that for many long wonderful minutes as barriers they had both erected came tumbling down. But at last he pulled back, so that he could see her face, and look into her eyes.

'Love me half as much, sweet Lydie?' he needed to know.

She felt shy suddenly, but he loved her. She knew then that he would not lie to her about that. 'M-more than that,' she whispered shakily.

'My darling,' he breathed, and tenderly kissed her. Joyous loving seconds passed. 'Say it,' he pulled back to request. 'Say it again.'

'What?' she asked huskily.

'You said, ''You know I love you?'' That's seared into my brain, into my heart, and I shall never forget it—I'm still getting over the almighty shock to hear you say what I have so craved to hear. May I not hear it again?'

Shyly, she smiled at him. 'I love you so, Jonah Marriott.' She pushed through an unexpected barrier of reserve to tell him, and, when he held her up close to him once more, 'I feared so that you might see—and there I went, blurting it out.'

'I'm so glad you did,' he murmured against her ear.

Lydie pulled back this time. 'Would you have told me, if I hadn't slipped up?'

Jonah placed a tender kiss on her upturned face and, looking adoringly into her shining green eyes, 'I was hoping we would grow closer on our honeymoon, hoping I could earn a little of your love,' he owned.

'You have it all,' she whispered, and was soundly kissed in exultation.

She had no idea they had moved until she found she was seated on a sofa with Jonah, one of his arms around her, one hand holding her hand.

'Oh, sweet, sweet Lydie, how you brighten up my day.'

'Do I?'

'Did I not tell you?' Lydie shook her head. 'I've wanted to, so many times. Little love, since knowing you again I've come to know that I only come alive inside when you are there.'

What a wonderful thing to say. 'I love you so,' she said softly, spontaneously.

Jonah beamed her the most sensational smile. 'That's all I've longed to hear.'

'Truly?' she asked breathlessly.

'Truly,' he answered. 'I've ached so.'

'Me too,' she confessed. 'When did you know?'

'That I was in love with you?' The answer was in her eyes, and he smiled gently, and quietly began, 'It was that Friday that your dear great-aunt died. You were supposed to be coming here for the weekend. I'd had business not far away from Beamhurst Court and, while I wasn't fully ready to acknowledge it, I couldn't wait to see you. All I had to do was make a small detour and I could enjoy seeing you sooner. Respecting your wish that I kept away from your home, I waited, about to ring on my car phone to find out if you were still home. But suddenly what do I see but you flying along—in totally the wrong direction.'

'You were furious,' she recalled.

'I was outraged,' he agreed. 'I have never in my life felt so churned up.'

'Because I was going in the wrong direction?' she teased gently, loving that she was able to do so.

'Because when I caught up with you, you said you weren't coming to Yourk House, and I saw your overnight bag in the back of your car. You were obviously spending the weekend with some-one—someone who wasn't me.'

'You thought...'

'I thought you were going to spend *our* week-end with some other man.'

'Charlie?' she asked faintly.

'None other. I have never, ever been so crazed with jealousy. It hit me so hard! I was jealous and, I knew then, hopelessly in love.'

'Oh, Jonah!' she sighed softly. And, as she thought of that day, 'I knew that same night, at the hospital, that I was in love with you.'

'Sweet darling,' he breathed, and held her close, and kissed her tenderly, and held her close again.

'That was weeks ago! All these weeks and neither of us knew!'

'I was afraid to tell you how it was with me,' Jonah owned, looking deep into her eyes.

'Afraid?' she prompted gently, and Jonah settled her into his arms, her head against his shoulder.

'I'd kissed you, the day after your great-aunt had died, and you'd pushed me away.' Lydie remembered; it had been a wonderful kiss. 'And I knew then that I was going to have to take it very slowly with you.'

'That kiss turned my legs to water,' Lydie confided, and, when Jonah pulled back his head in disbelief and looked into her face, 'I wanted to kiss you back,' she further confided.

'So you pushed me away?'

'I had to—I was drowning—and, well—um—you weren't the only one to become acquainted with the demon jealousy.'

'You were jealous?' He looked incredulous—but delighted.

Lydie smiled self-consciously. 'I couldn't help thinking that you'd probably have your arms around some other woman that very night.'

Jonah smiled into her face. 'What a joy you are,' he said softly, and kissed her. 'I'm going to have to stop doing that,' he said a moment later. 'Your tempting lips are wrecking my sanity. Love me?'

'So much.'

'Oh, my love.'

'All these weeks…'

'We've loved, and not known,' he ended for her. 'And there was I, impatient, yet fearful you might marry someone else before I could get you to agree to marry me. As I saw it then, I had to act, and act fast.'

'You told my father that you wanted to marry me.'

'It was the truth.'

'Oh, Jonah!' She sighed. If she was dreaming, she never wanted to wake up. 'But—you didn't feel you could tell me—um—how you felt?'

'How could I, my darling? You hadn't shown the smallest sign of caring for me. Hell, I'd kissed you—you'd pushed me away. Then there was Charlie ever-present.'

'Charlie?'

Jonah smiled. 'Nerves were getting to me—any man who looked at you was a threat. I wanted you. To my mind there wasn't time for me to come courting. You were proud; that fifty-five thousand stood between us. What was the point of my trying to date you? That fifty-five thousand would always be there.' Lydie stared at him in amazement. All this had gone through his head! 'To tell it how it was, Lydie,' he continued, 'I was running scared that someone else would get you.'

'Oh Jonah,' she whispered.

Gently he placed a kiss on the corner of her mouth, pausing to gaze at her beautiful face before going on, 'I wasn't sure you would swallow that line about your father preferring to owe money to someone inside the family...'

'But you tried anyway—and it worked.'

He grinned. 'It worked. But I knew, when you tried to find an ''out'' to say no, that it was too soon to tell you of the depth of my feelings for you. You said it would be cheating to marry me if you could find the money to pay me back, but

I couldn't tell you that I was cheating you by not telling you of the proposition I had just put to your father. And if I needed more evidence that you weren't thrilled about marrying me, then I didn't need to look further than when, while accept me you did, you made no bones about telling me you didn't want my kisses.'

'Oh, Jonah, did I hurt you?'

He smiled. 'It started to get better.' And, when she looked at him questioningly, 'About a fortnight ago?' he hinted.

She stared at him a second or two longer, then went a delicate shade of pink. 'When we came here so I could get away from our two mothers sending me potty.'

'It was a wonderful weekend. While I'd been working all hours, afraid to find time to see you more than briefly in case I blurted out how much I cared for you, I at the same time became desperate to see you, to spend some time with you.'

'It was the same for me,' Lydie confessed. 'I couldn't wait for that Friday.'

'Little love!' He kissed her because he just had to. 'It was a perfect weekend. Up until then you had shown all too plainly that you didn't even want me to kiss you.'

'We did kiss, didn't we?' she softly reminisced.

'Oh, we did,' he agreed, his eyes on her lovely mouth. 'It was wonderful. Though I'd still no intention—with our wedding so close—of blowing it all by telling you of my feelings.' He paused, then added, 'And when I rang you from Sweden on Wednesday, and you coolly suggested that ours wasn't the normal head-over-heels thing, I was glad I hadn't—even if I did feel a bit defeated.'

'Defeated?'

'Defeated, and not knowing where in blazes I was. For me, my darling, it was, and is, a head-over-heels thing. But there you are, dropping me down one moment and the next raising my hopes again. Making my heart lift by telling me ''I wish you were here'', only to crush my hopes by as good as telling me the only reason you wanted me there was because of the amount of luggage you had to transport.'

Lydie looked at him, stars shining in her eyes. It seemed incredible to her that anything she said should have such an effect on him. 'I meant it about wishing you were there, with me,' she confessed. 'The words just slipped out, and I had to hurriedly use the amount of my luggage as a cover in case you thought I was coming over all—um—personal.'

His smile broke through, and, as though that word 'personal' was some kind of a signal, Jonah stood up, taking Lydie with him. And, looking adoringly down at her, he then gently kissed her. 'It's been a long day, dear wife,' he said softly, and, picking her up in his arms, 'Unless you've any strong objection, I suggest it's time for bed.'

A delicate pink began to flush her skin, but she smiled as she shyly answered, 'I've no objection at all, dear husband.'

Looking down into her face, Jonah laughed softly in delight. And, his head coming nearer, 'Don't worry about a thing, sweet love,' he breathed against her mouth, 'I shall be with you.'

He carried her to the stairs, kissed her again, lovingly, lingeringly, and together they ascended.